The Scarlet Ribbon

The Scarlet Ribbon

DERRY O'DOWD

The
History
Press
Ireland

For Christine Patterson O'Dowd

First published 2012

The History Press Ireland
119 Lower Baggot Street
Dublin 2
Ireland
www.thehistorypress.ie

British Library Cataloguing in Publication Data.
A catalogue record for this book is available from the British Library.

ISBN 978 1 84588 729 2

Typesetting and origination by The History Press
Printed in Great Britain
Manufacturing managed by Jellyfish Print Solutions Ltd

Acknowledgements

With thanks to Ronan Colgan for saying yes, Beth Amphlett for being so lovely to work with, Katie Beard for the beautiful cover, and the whole team at The History Press for their efforts and dedication to *The Scarlet Ribbon*.

To Samantha Fanning, James Wagstaff and Deirdre O'Dowd for reading early drafts.

To Eoin Purcell for his advice.

And to Vanessa O'Loughlin for her unwavering support and wise counsel.

I

To bring away the afterbirth
Pour the oil of juniper into a glass of fine Spanish wine. Three dozen drops should be sufficient to excite the internal muscles and thus help to expel the placental cake and other remnants of the birth. Get the woman to drink it all.

Quinn Household Recipes and Remedies Book

DUBLIN, 1737

'You had no right to call for Surgeon Stone,' hissed the midwife, wringing her hands in agitation, plump cheeks flushed with anger. 'Physician Ryan will be most displeased!'

'Oh do be quiet, O'Grady. Can you not see how much pain and distress she is in? The purge has done nothing but make her soil herself; the afterbirth is still stuck within her. And what do I care for the pompous Ryan?' midwife Hayes whispered back, looking at the prosperous banker's young wife laying bloody and bruised on the tousled bed.

As O'Grady readied herself to make a scandalised retort, Mrs Butler moaned softly, and the midwives rushed to her side.

'My baby,' she moaned. 'My baby. Oh I should never have looked on the neighbour's child with his poor little face all but disfigured by a birthmark when I was pregnant; I knew it was a bad portent! I could not help myself, I put my hand to my cheek in shock and so my own child must suffer the same fate; she in turn will be marked on her face at the place where I put my hand to mine. This is my punishment.' And she turned her face to the wall and began to weep.

Midwife Hayes hitched up her skirts and knelt on the fine flagstone floor by the woman, taking her hand, talking to her softly as she would to a child, while her colleague looked on from the foot of the bed.

'Now my dear, look at me,' she pushed Mrs Butler's lank fair hair from her clammy forehead and looked into her wide blue eyes, glassy with tiredness after the lengthy labour. 'That is nothing but a fancy, like the way you wanted candied violets throughout your confinement; a fancy of the mind towards superstition as is the wont of pregnant ladies. Your daughter is safely with us and suckling contentedly on her wet-nurse with not a blemish nor mark in sight. Your emotions and actions while pregnant had no effect on the baby you carried. She is fine, but your afterbirth is firmly lodged. You just have a little more work to do and all will be well. Close your eyes and try to rest, good girl.'

As the midwives waited for the surgeon they lit more candles and banked up the fire, replaced the soiled sheets with clean ones and had more fresh water and linen fetched to the birth chamber, tongues silent, eager not to be overheard arguing as they could forfeit their fees.

A knock at the door disturbed them from their reveries and Midwife Hayes' face broke into a smile of welcome as she saw the grey-haired surgeon and his tall young assistant enter the room.

She rushed to fill them in on all that had happened, and O'Grady, annoyed at being left as an onlooker, quietly left the room to go downstairs and fetch the physician.

'James, help me if you please,' asked Surgeon Stone, and James Quinn nodded silently, waiting to be told what to do and pushing a tumbled dark curl away from his eyes.

Stone made his way to the side of the bed to speak to Mrs Butler. 'Now, my dear, we are here to offer whatever help we may. There is no cause for worry or alarm. Midwife Hayes here will hold your hand while James and I come to your aid.'

'Will it hurt?' asked Mrs Butler in a small voice, working the sheets around her fingers, her face as pale as the bedding she lay on.

'We will be our most gentle, I promise you.'

He bent down and felt her forehead before straightening up.

'Midwife Hayes, where is Mrs O'Grady?'

'I don't know, sir,' she replied, bewildered.

'Ah well, I don't suppose it matters much now there are three of us here. James, if you stand by me as I kneel and watch what I do.' So saying, the surgeon knelt by the side of the bed, pulled back the sheet and pressed his fingers onto Mrs Butler's belly.

She squirmed under the pressure and he apologised, his eyes making amends where words may have failed. He stood and made his way to the end of the bed, where he knelt down once more.

'James, come to me. Midwife Hayes, if you would stay by Mrs Butler and offer her whatever help you may.'

With everyone in place, Stone pulled the bedclothes up and then the birthing gown. He nodded to the midwife and she pressed the woman's hand. He pulled gently at the length of the grey birth cord that lay on the sheets between Mrs Butler's legs and she cried out in pain.

Still he pulled, and some of the afterbirth came away in his hand, with a great rush of blood. The screams ended abruptly as Mrs Butler gave way to a swoon.

'Damn!' swore the surgeon. 'I am going to have to put my hand up through the birth canal to get to the remainder of the placental cake. It is just as well she has fainted as this would be very distressing to her. Midwife Hayes, if you would be so kind as to keep holding her hand and talking to her gently even though she is not aware. James, wipe my forehead if you will, and there is blood in my eye.'

Stone eased his fingers up, until his entire hand was inside the woman and his face was a study of concentration as he tried to grasp the remains of the afterbirth and pull it away. The strain soon showed on him, and his hair became darker as he sweated freely.

'James,' he said, sitting back on his heels and removing his hand, wrist and forearm from the woman, 'I cannot reach it; you will have to try. I will guide you.'

The surgeon stayed kneeling by his pupil, nodding his encouragement, speaking softly, explaining what James needed to do, and casting glances at Mrs Butler who was still in a dead faint.

'I have it in my hand,' whispered James to Stone after a little time, and he pulled the bloody remains of the afterbirth through the woman's birth canal and onto the sheets.

'Thank God,' breathed Stone, 'she will recover.'

'Well, well, well,' came a furious voice from the door.

The three by the bed looked up in alarm, and saw Physician Ryan with Midwife O'Grady smirking by his side.

'Cover that woman with a sheet and get off your knees. You midwives get out of here. You may see to Mrs Butler when I am done talking to Stone and whoever this young man is.'

Ryan waited imperiously for the midwives to leave the room, the candlelight making the costly buttons on his jacket and waistcoat glow warmly, the black ribbon at the nape of his wig perfectly tied, a hand caressing the top of his gold-headed cane.

Once the door had been closed behind them, he faced Surgeon Stone, wrath written all over his face, the outside of his nostrils white with anger.

'It is just as well I have left Mr Butler in his study drinking cherry brandy to welcome his new child. He is a close friend and I promised that all would be well. And it was until you arrived here – who called you?' he barked.

'Does it matter?' asked Stone, pulling down the sleeves of his shirt. 'The purge had not worked and the afterbirth was still not delivered.'

'Do not presume to tell me my business, *surgeon*,' replied the physician, his face mottled with ill-suppressed rage. 'I administered a purging medicine, which would have worked had you waited.

'And who is this youngster, and why do I walk into a room to see him with his hand inside the privities of a most delicate woman? It is shocking that you would do this, shocking. A disgrace!'

'This is James Quinn, newly qualified surgeon and my assistant.'

'And tell me, Quinn,' said the physician, fixing the young man with a stare, 'how is it that I see you in such a position, ignoring the treatment of someone as myself?'

James took a breath to answer, but Ryan continued, jabbing his finger into the soft material of the apprentice's blood-spattered shirt, 'This is unnecessary meddling with midwifery at its worst. Men should not tamper so; female midwives are allowed to do so, but men such as myself will not touch and defile a woman of fine birth – or any woman for that matter – as you have, but rather treat her with medicine!' the physician's voice quavered in anger.

'I was just assisting,' replied James.

'Assisting!' shouted the physician, before lowering his voice as the woman on the bed stirred. 'You, sir, are no better than a barber-surgeon and should return to your business of cutting hair and lancing boils. Do not think this an end of the matter, sir. Stone, I wish you a good day. You may leave.'

2

To make a Marriage Pie

Clean a suckling pig, a young calf and a callow deer. Slice
the flesh nicely and put into a pie with oysters, salt, pepper,
the yolks of twenty boiled eggs and a good serving of
butter. Put in some water to keep it all nicely moist, and
place it in the fire until you smell that it is cooked.

Quinn Household Recipes and Remedies Book

James Quinn had just negotiated the eel-slippery rain-
soaked cobbles and turned the corner to the street where
his parents' home stood, when a blur of chocolate brown
stalled him and his horse.

James looked down and a pair of brown eyes regarded
him, stubby tail wagging in rapturous welcome.

'James! Finn knew you were coming, he has been waiting
all this time,' panted his sister Kate, looking most unladylike
with her ruby embroidered skirts and sepia petticoats all
rucked up with the effort of chasing the dog, pretty face
flushed, hair in disarray.

James dismounted in one fluid movement, picked up the
small dog, which proceeded to wet his face further with his
tongue, and pulled his sister to him in a hug.

'Fine as it is to see you James, you smell,' she smiled up at him, pushing dark, wet tresses out of her eyes.

'Well hello, and look at who it is!' remarked Mother Quinn, not pausing for breath. 'And you, Kate Quinn, supposed to be a young lady, running in the street with your skirts up where people can see you! James, was there nowhere along the way to clean yourself up? And us with your dinner guests arriving soon to plan your wedding, well I don't know. Make sure to leave that dog out too, with the horse, till he dries.'

'Hello, Mother,' James smiled and hugged her.

He closed his eyes and let his shoulders relax, content in Mother Quinn's embrace. His back hurt, his buttocks hurt, his thighs hurt. He could smell himself too, a mixture of leather and horse. He ran a hand across the dark stubble that covered his jaw and smiled wryly.

It had been a weary couple of days for the man and his horse, and much land had been covered. From the finery of the streets of the better parts of Dublin where he had studied surgery, through the lush rolling countryside, and on to the coarse scrubby land of Connacht with its straw-coloured grasses and trees bent like arthritic old men trying to make their painful way home over the open, wind-swept plains.

The sky had been leaden from the start; blackened, relentless and unceasing it seemed in the task of soaking everything beneath.

Fragments of the argument with Physician Ryan tormented him as he travelled; worries about his mentor Surgeon Stone who wanted him to take on the role of man-midwife even though the physician had been so disdainful of the men involved with the process of birth.

Stone's workload was too great for a man of his years and he had asked James to take on his man-midwifery tasks. Thoughts of his betrothed, Marguerite, who held his heart in the palm of her small hand. All three jostled for space so he felt that he might scream. But finally he had passed the fortified walls and came into sight of the bustling, prosperous coastal trading city of Galway that drew him closer to home.

His mother smiled at James and, taking his face between her hands, looked up into his eyes and kissed him. 'Now, away with you to freshen up. Your father is out seeing to a patient and our guests will be here soon.'

'Thank you, Mother, for the *Quinn Household Recipes and Remedies Book*. I know how long it has taken you to collect and put everything together.'

'Well now, son, you are welcome, but show me your thanks by doing as I say.'

James smiled as he turned away. He may be a grown man now, but he was always his mother's child first.

Once he had washed, James sat in his father's study, surrounded by the medical texts that Doctor Dara turned to for answers to perplexing questions. He remembered sitting here on his father's knee, demanding explanations of the curious drawings contained within the books, his father's deep chuckle and prediction that he, little James, would be a doctor too one day. The memory brought a smile to James's face.

'It is right that you are happy son, and happy I am to see you,' beamed Doctor Dara as he left the door to stride across the room to hug James.

His face, with copious unfashionable whiskers and kindly blue eyes behind spectacles, seemed a little more wrinkled than usual to his son. James banished the cloudy thought as he hugged his father back.

'We can talk later, son, and you can tell me all your news, but now your future family are due to call.'

At that moment, father and son heard a hearty welcome.

'God be with you all!' boomed Thomas Lynch as he swept into the Quinn hallway accompanied by his wife and children.

'My Lord, it's hot,' Thomas complained and touched his lips to Mother Quinn's cheek. 'May I seek your permission, dear lady, to banish this wretched thing from my head? And so, here is my new soon-to-be son-in-law home,' he continued, removing his wig while he talked, as James came down the stairs and past the assembled family to the girl in silken dove-grey damask.

'Marguerite.' He had never loved anyone with such passion. 'Marguerite.' He took her gloved hand. 'Marguerite.' He gazed at her, taking in the simple pearls at her throat and ears, hair a dark profusion, brown eyes full and sparkling bright at the happiness of seeing him.

All he wanted to do was gather her to him and never let go, but a discreet cough from behind disturbed him from his reverie and he dropped her hand.

'Well, son,' said Doctor Dara, resting his arm on James's shoulder, 'let's eat and get your marriage details finalised – it's so much easier to plan on a full stomach, I find!'

'Later,' James whispered to Marguerite, 'when all of this is done, it will be just you and me, my love.'

The following day, James sat with his father in the study.

'I just don't know what to do,' he complained.

'Ah James, it is only a matter of a bad-tempered, disapproving, pompous, well-appointed man who lives in the past in the case of Ryan. He does not like to see a man doing what he perceives to be a woman's work.

'Without you Mrs Butler would surely have died. You can overcome people like Ryan. As for the other? Stone is a good man and would not recommend man-midwifery as a career for you if he felt you would not be up to the task. It is obvious he needs your help at cases, and in return he offers the chance for you to study at the renowned Hotel Dieu in Paris to learn the craft.'

Doctor Dara paused and saw his son's face, which looked confused and very young. He patted James's knee, 'All will be well, son. You can take a little time to decide, and we can talk further. And, now, here is a small gift for you.'

His father rose and took two leather-bound journals from the cupboard that sat in the corner of the room.

James took them and smiled, 'Thank you, Father, you truly are a mindreader; they are just what I need. I would like to record a copy of all my correspondence, medical notes and everyday observations, and these journals will be perfect.'

Dara sat again and leaned forward, speaking softly. 'James, I have some bad news, son. It's Liam, Liam O'Flaherty. He died this morning'.

The news was not unexpected but James was saddened. He had a sudden memory of sunny summers when Liam had brought him out in his boat to lift lobster pots.

'You knew he had a bad chest and was ailing for a long time. He began to cough up a lot of blood. His appetite went and he just faded away. No treatment could save him.' Dara paused and relit his pipe, the watery sunlight in the room painting everything a weak yellow. 'You might like to visit his family.'

James took his leave and looked back to see white smoke from the pipe curling around his father's head. He lifted his hand in farewell, but Dara was absorbed in thought as Finn slept at his stockinged, slippered feet.

James rode out through the city's fortifications, past the quays and genteel living, over the bridge and into the rows of poor thatched cottages and unkempt streets that made up the Claddagh fishing village.

Untended boats floated idly at anchor in the cove and swans kept guard like white angels on the grey water while the fishermen paid their last respects to Liam O'Flaherty.

James made his way to the O'Flaherty cottage and knocked at the rough wooden planks that made up the front half-door, bleached to a powdery white colour by the wind and rain that came often and suddenly in the area, its knots looking like sullen, unblinking eyes. The door was badly warped; it squeaked noisily and had to be opened forcibly.

The face of a pretty young girl on the cusp of her teenage years, with curling auburn hair and blue eyes looked out. He pulled her name out of his memory.

'Carissa?' James asked.

She nodded.

'I am so sorry about your father,' he continued and then, seeing her blank stare, realised that she spoke little English and reverted to her native Irish tongue.

She did not smile or answer but stood aside to let him pass.

Inside the cottage, Liam's body was laid out on a scarred wooden table.

A handmade woven cross of straw lay on his chest and candles flickered smokily at his head and feet, filling the tiny space with the smell of fat and blocking out the light that filtered in through the mean window.

James hated these occasions, as they brought to mind the frighteningly quick illness and death of his tiny sister, born too early.

He stood by the body, remembering, sending a prayer to the heavens for his friend, and only then looked around the room. Carissa stood, head bowed, her younger sister Aileen by her side.

'Where is your mother?' he asked. He was startled by the knock at the door in the too-silent room, and as Carissa went to answer it, Aileen took him by the hand and drew the flimsy curtain back from the alcove by the ash-grimed open fireplace to show her mother lying there, not moving, gaze fixed on the rough beamed ceiling. He heard Carissa welcome in more mourners, and closed the curtain again as he sat on the shelf with Liam's widow.

She turned her head and looked at him, helpless, grief weighing her down, with eyes brimming and too bright with unshed tears. He helped her to sit up and held her close, whispering endearments all the time in an attempt to stem her sorrow. He rocked her gently, and some time later heard the mourners leave, muttering their sadness.

Their quiet was disturbed when Carissa pulled the curtain back. James left the widow to her private agonies and stepped into the room once more.

His heart went out to the girl. The fire had burned down, but he could see that she had tidied up as best she could for her father's wake.

'Carissa? Where are the little ones?' he asked, talking of her four younger siblings that ranged in age from toddler upwards.

'They are with the neighbour, for my mother needed some rest and Aileen and I thought it best that they would not be underfoot as so many people have come to see father. They do not understand, but know enough to be heartbroken.' She turned her head so he would not see the tears that were her constant companion. 'We will get them home later.' She angrily brushed her tears aside and sniffed, rubbing her nose on her sleeve.

'Your mother will be fine, Carissa. And the little ones are lucky to have a big sister such as yourself. I will get my own mother to come and see you from time to time. She is a good friend to me; if you let her, I am sure in time she will be one to you.'

He took his leave and held his hand up in farewell to the two young girls framed in the rotting doorway, one dark head, the other light.

The night of his wedding, James Quinn beamed to himself as he took in his new wife's slumbering form.

'Oh wake up, my love, my lover wake up,' James whispered softly into Marguerite's ear, 'oh wake up, my love, my lover wake up.'

'James, are we late? What's happening?'

'Nothing like that,' he smiled and kissed her warm, sleep-tousled hair. 'That was the happiest day of my life. What a day, and now my wife, where were we?'

She smiled coyly and her lip trembled just a little as she was suddenly shy of her new husband. She chided herself and twirled a strand of her hair around her finger – wasn't this the man she had known since childhood, they had played together, she knew each plane of his handsome face like she knew her own.

'I'm sorry I slept, James. I was so tired after it all.'

He smiled at her and helped her from the bed where she had lain down to refresh herself but instead had fallen into sleep. 'I loved every moment of the day,' he said with a smile in his voice, 'and what a future we have in store, Mrs Quinn. Now come to the candle so I can see you more clearly.'

He took her gently by the hand and continued talking to ease the nervousness he felt coming from her. He knelt before her and undid the ribbons on her boots and eased them off her feet. He lifted her foot, turned it, and kissed the sole gently.

'There were so many people to see me off. They gave me flowers and wished us well.' He let her foot be, stood and appraised her bodice, eyes crinkled and brow furrowed in concentration as he noted the pins, ribbons, hooks and eyes that he needed to undo to get closer to her.

'As we waited in St Nicholas' church for you, my mother took my hand and squeezed it tightly.' He pulled the ribbon, undid the pins and hooks – smiling at the memory of his mother's welling eyes – and laid them on the table by the bed.

'When the choir started singing,' he hummed 'Welcome, Welcome Glorious Morn' under his breath as he helped her walk out of her skirt, 'I saw you come up the aisle with your gown shining in the sun that filtered through the stained-glass windows, colouring your every step with all the shades of the rainbow, and I felt sure my heart would stop.'

He gently tugged down her petticoat and she stepped out of it.

'Then you were mine to the strains of "If Music be the Food of Love" and I was never prouder or happier.'

He eased her out of the embrace and paused as he helped her out of her hoop and she pushed it free with one foot.

He undid the ribbons on her stays and paused as he knelt once more before her. He traced his hand up her leg and took off her garter, and then the other one. 'Your father was funny; it was obvious he had been enjoying his own wares before he gave his speech – but then what is being a wine trader if you can't enjoy your own stock?'

He looked at her again. Her stomach skipped and she drew in a sharp breath as she saw his eyes darken as he knelt down. He smiled widely, and as his dimples showed he gently rolled down her silk stockings.

'My father was so proud he just had to sing. Then he told me he could never have wished for another daughter as good, kind and beautiful as you. They all love you, Marguerite.' He got up and she stood before him in her chemise in the candlelight.

James Quinn faced her, blood pumping, heart soaring. He put his hand on her waist and drew her nearer, whispering her name.

With trembling hand he pulled gently on the scarlet ribbon that held the neckline of her chemise and as it came loose, so too did the last whisper of sheer linen that covered her creamy skin. She stepped out of the garment, no longer shy, as the love of him took her by surprise and gave her strength.

'And now we are here, and you are mine, and I love you,' he whispered, and turning his head he blew out the candle.

Catching sight of her naked shoulders, he put the ribbon in her hand, murmured into her hair that he would treasure her forever and lowered his lips to hers.

3

To ensure an easy childbirth

Drink this up to six weeks before the child is due,
morning and evening, about half a pint each time but no
more. Boil a pretty amount of raisins and figs in a good
amount of fresh water; liquorice and aniseeds should be
added. Take from the heat when the mixture bubbles,
strain it off and drink the amount recommended once
it is cooled.

Quinn Household Recipes and Remedies Book

Dublin, 11 April 1738

Dear Father and Mother,

*In response to your last letter, yes, Marguerite is well, and we are
both delighted at the thought of being parents this summer. I have
not only married a woman who is kind and clever and beautiful,
but one that I love deeply, so I am a very happy man. And soon
to be a father! Thank you again for the recipes, Mother. Marguerite
is already buying in raisins to take as part of the remedy you have
recommended.*

*All goes well here. I am busy with my work and Laurence Stone
continues to teach me the way of helping in childbirth. I have asked*

for the assistance at Marguerite's birth from Midwife Hayes. I am sure I mentioned her to you already, and Marguerite's mother will come too.

Marguerite's aunt and uncle Sarah and Bernard Lynch have been most kind, and we are living in a fine home they have rented to us at a very good rate.

Perhaps I will buy the house from them once my own practice is established, but for the time being their help is much appreciated as I attempt to make a name for myself in Dublin.

We went to the Lynch house on Coote Lane, just by Trinity College, last Sunday for tea and to be introduced to some prominent members of Dublin's citizenry, and the talk of course fell to Marguerite's condition and the upcoming birth. The one name mentioned I never expected to hear on recommendation was that of Physician Ryan, but then he moves in such elevated company that I suppose I should not be so surprised! I have not come across him again as yet, and hope it stays that way for quite some time. I have taken your advice, Father, and am keeping a clear mind with regard to my medical future, but for now am enjoying my surgery and attendance at occasional midwifery cases.

And saying so, I am due at Stone's home shortly, so with your forgiveness I will sign off here and remain, as always, your loving son,

James.

Dublin, 20 June 1738

My own dear Mama,
I hope this little letter finds you well. Please be sure to give my fondest love to Papa and everyone else as I may well forget to say it again at

the end of my ramblings! This pregnancy has made me forgetful.

And large! Mama, you wouldn't believe how large I am getting, I wonder if I can get bigger still in the short time that is left before the arrival of my baby.

I shall refer to him or her from now on as 'darling', as my poor hand is tired already, even though I have only written a few short lines to you. My whole self is constantly a bit tired as I am not sleeping very well; darling keeps me awake with his or her tumbling at night when I am so eager to close my eyes and drift off into sleep.

As to names, James decided on Daniel for a boy, as strong as the Daniel in the Bible stories. While I chose Jasmine, as sweet and beautiful as the flower, should we have a girl – how frivolous of me, Mama, but that is how I feel, frivolous and happy when I am not crying at the slightest little thing.

I saw a mama bird with her little baby from the window earlier this morning and found it so beautiful that the tears sprang unbidden to my eyes. I can feel them dampening at the thought again so will not linger.

I find it hard to breathe, Mama. I sometimes think that darling needs more breath from me but perhaps that is my fanciful imaginings – of which I have many at the moment!

Heartfelt thanks for sending Peg here to me. It is like a little bit of home when I see her dark head and ready smile, and she is a marvel at running the household, especially as I am so indisposed at the moment. We didn't want to hire staff that were unknown to us, given my condition. I do not mean to call Peg a member of staff, for she was ever like a second mother to me.

Mama, my pretty shoes and boots no longer fit as my poor feet appear to be pregnant too! I am wearing Chinese slippers as I write – indeed they are my new favourite footwear.

This letter will be carried by Uncle Bernard's store manager – it will be with you within the week – and he has agreed to bring us back the Spanish trim for our carriage. Not that I am going out! I fear for my baby's safety, riding a horse or being jolted over Dublin's cobbles in our carriage. And the Dublin ladies would be sure to hold their noses in the air if I passed; the girl from the country who knows so little of their manners and customs. I miss Galway and the smiles of the people that I know and am comfortable with!

But I will not grumble, Mama, for I do not want to make darling sad – I am sure he or she can feel if I am sad and then I am sadder and can't help but cry all over again.

I am eagerly awaiting your arrival, Mama; James is often away and I am a little lonely. Do come as soon as you can – I couldn't bear for you not to be here for the arrival of my darling. I know that Papa and Doctor Dara and James's mama will be coming too, but it is your presence that I most desire.

Please write back as soon as possible to let me know when you will come – I am enclosing our new address as Aunt and Uncle Lynch have been constant in their kindness and insisted on renting one of their larger houses to us.

I can see St Patrick's Cathedral from where I sit and am sure that the angels are protecting me and my dear heart, and that comforts me greatly. Please thank Papa for arranging such a small rent with Uncle Bernard.

My dear Mama, another request, please. I will need a girl to help me with darling – do you know of anyone that would come here? Could you arrange it for me? I would dearly love a Galway girl, kind and giving of herself to myself and baby and who will not grumble when I may take her to task, although I am hoping I will not have to do that. A girl who is used to children – more used than me! But not so much that my darling would fall in love with her and not his or her mama, who will be a constant through life.

Much as I am tired now, I cannot wait to hold my own baby

and kiss his or her little head and look into his or her little eyes and profess my love, for I love my darling and I very much look forward to all the playing and cuddling and loving that we shall share.

I also enclose a pretty bolt of silk for you, Mama. It is apparently all the rage at the Season in London and will bring out the flecks in your eyes.

I hope, Mama, that the birth goes well – Aunt Sarah swears it will, thanks to our family's great success with birthing babies and my child-bearing hips – as I want to give my own darling heart brothers and sisters so that they can all play together, and I will not love one above the other but will share my love evenly so they each know I am theirs forever.

And now, my dear Mama, I am going to lie down, as James is ordering me to rest at least a couple of times every day.

I miss you, Mama. Hurry to my side to be with me when darling comes. I won't be selfish and hold him or her all to myself – well maybe I will a little, but I want you to have a share in my glorious baby too. My heart is stolen already and I have not yet met the dear heart who has robbed it.

I love you Mama, and will see you soon, until then I am your own dear daughter,

Marguerite.

The servant who arrived at the door was sweating and agitated. Peg showed him in and called for James.

'Well, man, out with it. What's the matter?' enquired James.

'There has been a terrible accident at the docks. You must come. The pulleys gave way and spilled a large load onto all that were standing below. They need you at the Infirmary now if you are to save any lives, that's what they told me. There is a lot of blood, and bones are on show.' The servant turned pale as milk as he relayed his breathless, grisly message, tripping over the words in his anxiety to get them out.

'You go on back,' replied James, 'and I will be there as quickly as I can.'

As the servant ran, James hurried up to Marguerite's bedchamber.

He entered the room and saw his wife lying amongst the pillows, pale. She felt that today was the day that their baby would arrive, so her mother had called for Midwife Hayes and her colleague Midwife Doyle.

Marguerite's face was puffy and swollen; indeed, her mother thought she had been crying copiously at the slightest thing that tugged at her heartstrings now that her time was so near. She was very restless, with an aching head and sick stomach.

Her mother had called for Physician Ryan three days earlier, as he had come so highly recommended from her sister-in-law. He had diagnosed an imbalance in her humours and advised bloodletting.

That first day, James had held her hand and watched as Ryan used the shining lancet to cut a vein in Marguerite's pale arm and her ruby blood had filled a pewter bowl until she fainted. He still did not like the man, and the physician's manner was cool towards James, but anything that would help his Marguerite would be done.

On her recovery the following day, she was purged with a foul-tasting medicine, her face puckered like a child's as she took it. After the violent, wet bowel movements had passed she felt improved, though her head still troubled her and her body felt swollen all over.

As James told her what had happened at the docks, she said, 'You go, my love. I am fine here with Peg and Mama, and the midwives shall be here soon. And before you know it we shall have our dear heart in our arms at last.'

'James, we will call for you as soon as anything happens, please go and see to those poor men and worry not,' Mama Lynch echoed her daughter, eyes smiling at him from under her dark tresses. 'We are all ready for the arrival of your son or daughter, everything is in hand. We will call for you if we need to.'

James smiled at her, picking up on her excitement. 'Marguerite, I love you, and I will see you soon with our dear heart. I love you more than my words can say, my darling.' Marguerite smiled up at him and his words. Then he kissed her lightly, left the room and ran to find the waiting carriage.

James arrived at the Charitable Infirmary very quickly, for though today was a special Feast Day of the Virgin Mary, the parades had not yet started and the bridge from the south side of the city to the north was still clear, so his coach had no trouble.

He entered the building and ran to the room where the injured had been taken. A scene of complete disorder met his eyes, men lay all about, the wooden tables stained with their blood, and cries of pain rang in his ears.

'Thank God you're here!' cried one of the surgical apprentices. James took a breath and crossed to the badly hurt sailor.

He ran his hands along the man's roughly broken leg, looked at the bloody, glistening bones and sinews that gaped through the torn skin, and realised that an amputation would be the only thing to save his life.

'Everything will be well now,' he whispered into the man's ear. 'Hold fast and we will help you as best we can.' The sailor's eyelids fluttered in reply and James turned to his two apprentices.

'Hand me an apron. Get the laudanum – this man needs to have his leg amputated if we are to save him from gangrene and putrefaction, and it will be necessary to dull his senses.' And for us to not have to restrain him so much, he thought to himself grimly.

The apprentices laid out a tourniquet, knife for skin and muscle, and a saw for the bone as James ran through the steps of the operation with them. Once the laudanum had been administered and the sailor was more restful, they put a lead ball into his mouth for him to bite on when the pain took him. They tied him to the table with leather restraints and James began to run through the operation in his mind.

Make a curved incision, incise the muscle, saw through the bone, catch and tie the bleeding vessels, let the skin flap cover the exposed bone and bind firmly, he thought.

'Well now, what do we have here?' a voice disturbed his mental inventory and James looked up to see Surgeon Stone return from treating another man badly injured in the accident, wiping his bloodied hands on his apron. He looked up, delighted and relieved to see his mentor, before attending to the task in hand once more.

Meanwhile, the sailor, clear terror in his eyes and in the sweat that coated his face and brow, was advised to bite down hard on the ball. The man lost control of his bladder and the warm stench of urine was added to the rich iron smell of his blood.

A tourniquet was tied tightly to the sailor's thigh, he was held down, and James raised the knife he was gripping tightly, lowered it and began the operation to the sound of the sailor's muffled screams.

Marguerite tossed and turned on the bed, her brow damp with moisture, dark hair sticking to the pillows with her sweat.

'There, my sweet,' crooned Peg, 'your little one will be with you soon. Take my hand and your mama's hand, and we will help you deliver your darling.'

'We love you, Marguerite,' said her mother, 'and would bear the pain for you if we could. We cannot, so take our strength and we will all do it together, my beautiful girl. We love you, we love you.'

The midwives stood at the foot of the bed, waiting, Hayes echoing what the other women said.

'Mama, my head hurts and I have a pain deep under my right breast, a different pain. My sight is clouded,' Marguerite cried, panicked and in distress.

'There, there, my sweet, sweet girl, shh, shh. We shall call for Physician Ryan again,' replied her mother as she looked at Peg and the midwives with concern in her eyes. 'And we shall get James home for you too, as his love and strength will add to ours and we will all get through this together, my darling girl. Then you will have your baby in your arms and forget that this had ever been a trial for you.'

Midwife Doyle nodded and left the room quietly and quickly as the others returned to their gentle ministrations.

The men were having difficulty restraining the sailor as James sawed through his bone. Sweating through the exertion of holding the terrified, suffering man and the raw noise of the saw against bone, James looked up and saw, for the second time that day, an agitated servant. From his own home. Marguerite. The baby surely wasn't here already?

He listened to the servant's explanation numbly, the sound rushing through his ears like the waves crashing onto Barna beach in the midst of a storm. Marguerite was in great pain and Physician Ryan had been called for again. Fear gripped his belly and he felt his insides soften and his vision darken and swim.

James looked at the bloody scene under his fingers. He nodded, told the servant that he would be back as soon as possible, and continued to work on the sailor. As the man started to bleed copiously, they tightened the tourniquet and James felt a sinking sense as he saw that this operation would take longer than anyone could have foreseen.

Marguerite was crying endlessly as the horrible pain coursed through her and took her breath away again and again. Rolling through every fibre of her being, a relentless crushing pain, like someone was sitting on her chest and beating her whole body. The pain came from deep within her, too. And then the pain was in her heart as she knew that she was very ill and something was dreadfully wrong.

Her heart cried out, hurting, hurting, and as the stars bloomed in her head and a dark blossoming took over her vision, she screamed, 'James!'

Then she began to convulse, jerking her heavily pregnant body like a badly controlled puppet, so badly, amazing in its viciousness and total sense of wrongness.

She foamed at the mouth, the white stuff dribbling down her chin, shocking to see. Red joined the white as she bit her poor tongue, unable to stop herself.

The women held on to Marguerite as one, to stop her falling from the bed with her precious cargo.

As the beautiful young woman breathed out heavily, everyone around her did too, thinking the bad time past. But then Marguerite's breathing ceased and a dusky hue stole over her face.

The midwives fell to their knees and started to pray. Peg began to cry and Mama Lynch stood in the whispering and sobbing of the close room, shocked beyond belief, looking at her baby girl who still carried her grandchild. The tears crept down her cheeks, leaving silvery tracks in their wake.

James finally managed to secure a carriage. The sailor had bled his life away, despite their best efforts, and James felt stricken that a life was lost. He sat on the edge of his seat in the carriage, desperate for it to go faster so he could get home to his Marguerite.

Marguerite started to breathe again. It was long and harsh, but she was alive, and the women were so relieved that a sense of joy filled the bedchamber.

'My love, my love, welcome back,' her mother smiled tremulously as she took her hand.

'Mama, I am so tired. And I have a terrible pain around my baby, Mama. Mama!'

Marguerite cried out in agony as a gush of blood stained the white sheets with dark red sorrow.

James stared at the serene face of the Blessed Virgin Mary, smile lifting her lips for eternity, fixed there by the sculptor. Masses of flowers covered the bower that the statue was carried on, in every colour under the sun. The faithful sang hymns to celebrate her Feast Day, their slow feet charting the progress of the procession. *Regina Caeli, Laetare, Alleluia*. Queen of Heaven, Rejoice, Alleluia; their voices carried by devotion up to the skies above.

James felt the sense of desperation again as he realised that his carriage was entirely stalled on the bridge. 'I have to go!' he shouted up to the driver, and took to his feet. He pushed past the crowds, desperate to be home, ignoring the pains from passing elbows in his great need to be with Marguerite. He was jostled and shouted at, and even kicked once or twice, but his gaze was firmly directed elsewhere, with his mind on his love.

Marguerite began to flail and jerk around her bed again. It was too small to hold her; she was like an animal trapped in a cage that was the wrong size. She foamed at the mouth, snarling, her head snapped from side to side, inhumanly.

'Oh dear, yes,' spoke Physician Ryan. 'I can see I am here too late. If you had only called me earlier,' he sighed and turned his palms outwards in emphasis, 'I may have been able to do something for her. Her mother fits are so severe that I fear there is nothing I can do. I'm afraid you must prepare your daughter and her child, your grandchild, for the next life.'

Marguerite slipped away from them then, into unconsciousness, as if she had heard the physician's words and there was nothing left to fight for.

Peg sank to her knees and took Marguerite's hand. Marguerite's mother knelt on the opposite side of her daughter, taking the other hand, crooning to her, baby soft words of love. Her tears fell to the bedclothes and wet the bump under Marguerite's white birthing gown, drops of baptism from a human font.

The midwives busied themselves with Marguerite, for they knew she was about to die the dreaded death of many young women, and wanted to save her unborn baby's soul. A baptismal tube was inserted through her birth canal, held open with a coin. Another coin was placed in her mouth so that the air might flow through to the little soul she still carried.

Lastly, the windows and door of the room were opened so that Marguerite's soul, and that of her baby, would not be trapped in the room and could fly to Heaven.

All James could hear was the sound of his own laboured breathing as he ran along the street. The cobblestones were uneven and slippery and he fell, again and again, hurting his hands and knees.

Ahead, he saw a black carriage pull away from his house. As it passed by, the passenger stared ahead grimly, his aquiline features barely visible in the gloom, a gold-headed cane clasped in his gloved hands. James realised he had missed Physician Ryan.

James ran into the house, bumping his shoulder painfully against the front door. He took the stairs two at a time, breathless, eager to see his wife and new child.

He came to Marguerite's bedchamber and stopped, for the door had been wide open to him, and he willed what he now knew to be true not to be so.

His wife lay quite still on her labour bed, partially covered with crimson-soaked sheets, her expectant belly undelivered. Peg knelt to one side of her, Mama Lynch to the other. Midwives Hayes and Doyle were praying at the end of the bed. All were weeping.

As James approached the bed he could see the baptismal tube that penetrated Marguerite's bloody, swollen birth canal. His breath came torn as he moved to her side. Her heart did not beat for him as his trembling hand touched her soft chest.

'How long? How long is she like this?' he demanded, but the women couldn't answer him, so great was their grief. He put his hands to his dead wife's pregnancy and stood back in amazement as he realised that there was still life within.

From the deep recesses of his memory James plucked greedily at the words of Laurence Stone, and he fumbled in his pocket and found the gift from his father, a Spanish pocketknife. He threw back Marguerite's birthing gown. The knife was in his hand. He slashed deep and long. Blood filled the wound. Deeper and deeper he went.

The women screamed at him to stop and he shook his head wildly, snarling at them.

Marguerite's womb appeared at last. Then thick meconium appeared in the wound, and there was the infant. James pulled hard. The newborn boy was blue and made no sound. James smacked his tiny, slippery feet to no avail. Grabbing the newborn by the ankles, he swung the child in an arc around his head. Crimson and dark green spattered the walls. Then, a feeble cry was heard.

'He lives,' said James, voice breaking.

'He lives? A boy? Oh James,' cried Mama Lynch and she rushed to his side, taking his son from him to clean and cuddle him.

As the sound of the baby's thin wails and the sob-soaked

coos of Mama Lynch filled the room, James looked to Marguerite.

Blood had trickled from the bed to the floor. His sorrowful eyes traced the dark red drip to the pool of mess in which the she lay.

Peg, weeping, left the room. The midwives, crying all the time, held her belly as he applied a binder. They prayed for her departed soul and for the future of her newborn baby as they tenderly cleansed the dead woman and cleared the soiled clothing and bedding. There was a great silence.

'Go, now,' he whispered hoarsely to the midwives, 'and thank you.'

He sighed from the core of his being, shoulders slumped in defeat, face pale, eyes burning. Midwife Hayes laid her hand on his shoulder as she left, but he did not feel her touch.

He lay down by Marguerite's side and gathered her gently to him as his tears streamed and wet her hair. He pushed the tresses back from her face and gently closed her eyes with trembling fingers. The scarlet ribbon that was part of her wedding finery was in her hand; she had wanted it with her during the birthing. He took it from her hand before death closed it there forever, and put it in his pocket.

James kissed her face, then, and not minding the mess of blood and fluids held her close to him, rocking her.

'Oh wake up, my love, my lover wake up,' he whispered softly into Marguerite's ear, 'oh wake up, my love, my lover wake up.'

And as his tears blinded him, and the sobs that hurt his throat and heart rolled relentlessly, James Quinn surrendered to his dead wife's last embrace.

4

To ease the sorrowful mind
Take a good handful of honeysuckle, sweet chestnut and
gorse and add to a fine amount of fresh water. Boil the
mixture until steam rises from it and the ingredients are
quite soft. Strain the mixture and leave to cool. Once
it is cooled add a few drops of rose water and a spoon
of sugar. Mix well and let it stand for a few days. Take a
couple of spoonfuls at any time when needed.

Quinn Household Recipes and Remedies Book

Peg smiled tentatively at James as she set his supper in front
of him. He stared down at the plate without seeing what
was on it, took up his fork, and put some of the food into
his mouth. It tasted like ashes on his tongue; everything did
these days, colourless and tasteless.

His stomach rolled uneasily, for in truth he was still ill
from last night's excess of brandy. He angrily blinked back
the tears that threatened and forced some more food past
his lips and onto his tongue. He swallowed like he was
eating stones instead of good food prepared with care, and
looked up to see Peg watching him intently.

'What is it, Peg? I am tired, late home again after treating the sick. What do you want?' he asked of her brusquely, wearily.

Her smile faltered, then she seemed to take stock of herself and cleared her throat as she said, 'Well, I was just wondering ...'

James motioned with a dismissive wave of his fork for her to go on.

'It's just that Baby Daniel is so gorgeous, now that he is six months old. And sitting unaided. And such a happy, sunny little person. Do come up to the nursery to see him. He is so peaceful as he sleeps, with his little lids and dark long lashes covering his great brown eyes. Why, he is even starting to make talk! He says "ba ba"; he is so pleased with himself, almost surprised at himself. Just this morning he said "ma ma".'

The words dried in her mouth as she faltered, and she looked at James anxiously. She had not meant to hurt him, but she knew that she had.

'I am too busy now, Peg. I have case notes to write all evening.'

'But, it is so long since you have set eyes on him, why—'

James cut her off mid-sentence and roughly pushed the table away from him, throwing the fork onto the plate with barely disguised irritation.

'It is no damn business of yours,' he hissed at her angrily as the chair scraped back across the floor. He stood and put his hands on the table, holding onto it tightly for support.

She left the room, frightened and hurt at his rough treatment of her. As she calmed herself she felt a great sorrow settle on her shoulders; for herself, for Marguerite, for the baby. And for James, who was suffering so greatly.

She sighed and put her hand on the banister to climb the stairs softly and slowly, with pity and sadness around her like a cloying, heavy cloak, wearing her down with its weight.

James Quinn set down his quill and looked at his case notes, the words blurring before his eyes. His eyes roamed around the room, with the leather-bound books lining the shelves, the candle on the desk making a pool of buttery light over his messily written pages. Marguerite sat here once.

He traced an ink-stained finger lightly along the top of the desk, as if he could take in some of her essence from the grain of the wood there. He looked up to the ceiling and sighed as the all-too-familiar grief fell on him again, crushing him. He was unable to catch his breath. He panicked and stood, not noticing in his haste to get to the brandy bottle that the chair he had been sitting on fell to the floor, clattering there and breaking the night's quiet silence with its jolting descent.

Peg stood at the door of the study, watching him drink his sorrow away. She had heard the chair falling and had known what he would be doing, he did it every night. Her heart went out to the man sitting on the floor by the desk, nearly empty bottle by his side. He was muttering as he sobbed.

The light from the desk's candle on his hair and face softened him and made him look younger – his son was so like him – and in that moment she opened the door, entered, and knelt down by him, heartsore and eager to help the man-child.

'Ah now, James, come and sit over here with me and tell me your woes.' She helped him up and they staggered over to the couch together. He raised his tear-stained face to hers and took another great drink from the bottle. He wiped his mouth on his sleeve and started to lay out his sorrows in front of her, scared little soldiers, as he had never talked to anyone about Marguerite's death before now.

'I can't believe that she is gone, you see. I don't believe it, I can't believe it, for then our love and our plans would all be lies. It was all a lie. Was it all a lie? I won't believe it, Peg. I won't.

'I asked God to give her back to me, the day we laid her down and I felt like I was watching over it. That I wasn't there. That is wasn't happening to me. I said to him, take the baby, give me back my wife.'

He heard Peg's sharp intake of breath and nodded sagely at her before continuing, shouting this time.

'I bargained with him and he didn't listen to me. The baby sleeps upstairs and my wife sleeps in the cold dark earth. I hate God for what he did to me, so I took to St Anne's churchyard where she is laid with a bottle in my hand and yelled to the night sky, cursing him. I drank there and then I pissed up against the door of the church – right there, Peg!' He bent his head and the tears dripped onto the back of his hands.

Peg sat mute in her shock. She couldn't speak. She remembered James's father, and Marguerite's, trying to prise him away from the poor girl lying on her deathbed that terrible night. He had pleaded with them, cajoled them, then begged them not to take her away from him.

Doctor Dara had tried his best, but he was unable to reach his son. He looked at Thomas Lynch; two grown men standing in the middle of that awful chamber with the tears streaming and the hurt eating their hearts at the sight of the beautiful dead woman and her husband who was wild with the unbearable sorrow of it all.

They had to fetch his mother, and only when he saw her would he let his wife go at last. James kissed Marguerite gently for the last time. He slid off the bed stiffly and fell to the floor, hurting himself again. He cried out for his mother.

She came to him, picked him up, and bundled him to her tightly. He knelt with his mother on the floor of the bedchamber, clumsily, his head on her shoulder, crying, taking in great gasps of air, soaking her hair with the tears that freely flowed down his face. She had rocked him and crooned to him, her kindly face furrowed in great distress. She stroked his hair and called him her baby, always her baby boy. But she couldn't answer him when he asked how he could go on without his wife.

Mother Quinn didn't know the answer; she realised she couldn't mend her son with her kisses and love this time.

'Then I felt guilty, Peg,' he continued his drunken confession, suddenly grasping her hands earnestly. 'You see, if I had only been there she wouldn't have died. I should have stayed, not gone to help at the Infirmary. My patient died anyway, so what use was I there? And if she had not been pregnant at all, then she would not be dead.'

His voice lowered to a whisper before rising again, 'It is the baby's fault, Peg, and that is why I do not want to see him! Do not ask me to see him! For he stole his mother's life. Stole his mother's heart, stole his mother's eyes, stole his mother's smile. He took her! And she's gone. She's gone.' He stopped, and with eyes closed fell forward onto Peg.

Peg eased herself out from under him and covered him with the blanket that was there from the night before. She turned off the light, righted the chair, took the empty bottle in her hand and closed the door behind her. Her mouth set in a grim line. Something needed to be done, and quickly. Over six months on and James was much worse instead of any better.

And the poor baby. God knows she loved Daniel, but she could not always play mother and father to him. She nodded to herself and set off to find her own paper, quill and ink.

Dublin, 20 December 1738

Dear Sir, Doctor Dara.

Please forgive me, but I truly felt you must know.

It is your son, James; he is not well. He cannot cope with his troubles. He is greatly distressed, doesn't eat or wash. He goes to his work, but returns like a wraith, a pale, shaking, imitation of himself, unshaven and smelling of last night's brandy. I know that you are grieving too, for we all loved Marguerite, love her still even now that she is gone. And I do not wish to add to your sorrows and burdens further, but I feel that I cannot cope alone any longer.

You see, he is drinking brandy heavily, every single day and late, late into the next. I am worried for I don't know what to do any more. I have tried, believe me, for I care for him. And I am more sorry for him and Marguerite than words can say. But he is not healing. I know it takes time. After the death of my own poor mother, rest her soul, it was a long time before I was right again. But his sorrow and grief are like nothing I have ever seen. It scares me and makes me helpless. I do not know what to do.

He is angry at everyone and at himself. I try to be patient with him when he is abrupt with me, but it is getting harder.

It would break my heart to leave my employ and Baby Daniel. And the saddest thing of all is that he will not look on his baby son. Will not touch or cuddle him, nor talk or sing to him. Indeed, he blames the baby most vehemently for Marguerite's death. He wants to send the baby away from him and out of his house and life.

Daniel is the sweetest thing, all innocence and smiles. Once I came to James with him, but he was in a drunken state, sprawled out. I came in with the baby and he held out his arms for his father. And his father paid him no mind and caused Daniel's little face to twist in confusion and then distress as James shouted at me to take him away. I left with the baby crying his little heart out.

So you see, sir, that it is with a very heavy heart indeed that I write to you. I wish to stay and see Daniel grow to the fine young man that he will be, and for your own son James to recover and return to the fine young man that he once was.

Sorrow and his brother grief are terrible burdens to bear, we know that, but they are making an empty man of your son, gaunt and hollow eyed. He will not listen to me, but I think he will listen to you.

Please come.

I am sorry for all that is happening and my own inability to cope with it, but your help is sorely needed here in Dublin. I cannot comfort him, perhaps you can.

Please take my best wishes to your wife and family.

Yours,
Peg Reilly.

Doctor Dara sat in his study. He held his spectacles away from his face and wiped his eyes. He took a breath, blew it out tremulously, picked up Peg's letter and read it again from the start, heart thumping uncomfortably.

He would have to go and see them all in Dublin. He had no idea how much worse things had become.

Damp bed sheets roped around his legs, James turned uneasily in his sleep.

All he could hear was the sound of his own laboured breathing as he ran along the street.

The cobblestones were uneven and slippery and he fell, again and again, hurting his hands and knees. He could hear a baby crying now, its thin, reedy cry filling the air. He ran faster then, smiling and eager to meet his new child.

He ran into the house, bumping his shoulder painfully against the front door. He took the stairs two at a time, breathless, eager to see his wife and baby, smiling. The baby's cries intensified and James's heart beat harder at the longing to hold it and Marguerite close to him, his new family.

He entered her bedchamber.

His wife lay quite still on her labour bed, partially covered with crimson-soaked sheets, her expectant belly undelivered.

'Where is the baby? I can hear it crying!' he shouted, and put his hands to his dead wife's pregnancy and stood back in amazement as he realised that there was still life within, that was where the cries were coming from.

He fumbled in his pocket and found the Spanish pocketknife. He threw back her birthing gown. The knife was in his hand. He slashed deep and long. Blood filled the wound. Deeper and deeper he went. He was sweating badly, he fumbled and the knife fell from his hand.

He reached for it again, the baby's cries spurring him on to work faster and faster to release it from the darkness of the womb.

James cut and cut again, deeper and deeper – was there no end to this? Where was Marguerite's womb? He paused, briefly, and wiped the sweat from his brow and eyes. The blood there left him blinded and he used his sleeve to clear his vision.

He was hacking now, desperate to get to the child within. Blood gushed, it was everywhere, he could make out nothing.

Marguerite's womb appeared at last. Then thick meconium appeared in the wound.

A cold hand wrapped around his ankle, tugging at his leg, pulling. He looked down and saw his wife lying on the floor, beautiful and urgent in her need.

'James, why are you not helping me? I will die, please help me!'

He looked to the bed again, perplexed. 'I am helping you, my love. See, here I am delivering you of our baby who is crying with the need to get out.'

He paused, knife in hand. The room was still, except for the baby's crying. He looked up past Marguerite's pregnant belly to see her face laying on the pillows. But it was not her laid there, her face did not greet him. It was the sailor from the Infirmary.

James awoke with a start, cold, so cold, sweating with the fear that gnawed at his insides. He threw the blanket off and lurched around in the dark, knocking things over, hands trembling until he found the bottle. He drank deeply, his need for it taking over everything else except for the empty aching deep inside. He took the brandy back to the settee with him, and sat with his knees up under his chin, arms clasped around them, rocking, sobbing and drinking until the morning came.

Father and son walked slowly. Doctor Dara had been in Dublin for two weeks now and wanted to return home to Galway. While he had loved seeing Daniel, his time with James had exhausted him emotionally and he longed to embrace his wife. The weak sunlight filtered through the tops of the trees, creating a new, young, bright green canopy overhead as they strolled on. Daffodils peeked their heads through the ground, crocuses too, on this spring morning.

'We'll stop here, James, if we may, and go into St Audoen's church. I want to rub the lucky stone – or lucky slab would be a better name for the great Celtic piece of granite – for my safekeeping on my journey back west. Not that I have anything of great value for the brigands to steal, I suppose,' he smiled and looked at his son, but James was far away from him. Doctor Dara sighed and pulled on James's sleeve. 'Come inside, son, and we can sit awhile out of the breeze.'

James followed his father into the church, everything in him rebelling, quailing at the thought of entering. He had not been inside a church since Marguerite was laid to rest, though he had been in a churchyard, he thought to himself with a pang of guilt.

He walked up the aisle with his father, their footfalls echoing around the still of the ancient church. Doctor Dara motioned to a pew and they both sat quietly, breathing in the serene nature of their surroundings. James wanted to bolt, leave the place and his father, find himself alone with his misery again. But as Doctor Dara cleared his throat James sighed; he knew his father was going to try to talk sense into him again, whatever that may be.

'Son, I know this has been a truly terrible time for you,' he paused, took off his spectacles and wiped them with the handkerchief he kept in his pocket for just that purpose before putting them back on again. 'It has been for all of us. Marguerite was such a beautiful young woman, warm, loving, giving. She stole all of our hearts. She would have made a wonderful mother had she been given the chance.'

He paused, cleared his throat and started to speak again, while James stared resolutely ahead, pale as one of the alabaster statues in the church as he looked through the window behind the altar.

'James, son, look at me now, take my hand.'

James turned slowly to face his father.

'I am so sorry, but she is gone, truly gone. Remember her; that is the best gift you could ever hope to give her. Love her, and that way you will always keep her memory alive.

'And James, no amount of brandy will bring her back, nor dampen your memories or hurt. You will only hurt yourself further if you carry on as you are. And Daniel, Peg and the rest of us too. You can weep an ocean, but don't drown in it.'

He cleared his throat once more, let go of his son's hand and looked ahead again. 'James, I must now talk of Daniel. It would be best if he stayed with you. A child, especially one without a mother, needs a father. Be his father. Be a father to him, son.

'I know you will love him. In time, perhaps, you will see his mother's features in him as a blessing, her final gift to you, and love him all the more for that instead of despising him for something that was not his fault. Your mother and I will not take him and raise him, he is yours. Yours and Marguerite's.'

Doctor Dara paused and smiled at the memory of Daniel's small, dimpled hand grasping his large one this morning as he took his leave, his solid, warm little body as he sat for a cuddle.

Peg was holding him, and the baby showed his new skill of waving his grandfather off, smiling and delighted with himself, the sight of a couple of tiny white pearly nubs of teeth coming through. Peg was happier too, he thought. Now if only he could help James.

His reverie was disturbed as a choir and musicians assembled for practice, and he glanced at his son. James still sat as unmoving as before.

As the joyful, triumphant, heraldic strains of the beautiful tune opened, and as the violins and trumpets resounded around the church, James stood and bolted.

His father caught him at the door and took his son's shaking body to his in a tight embrace. He stroked James's hair, well aware that the last time he heard the song 'Welcome, Welcome Glorious Morn' was at his wedding. The choir and musicians were plainly there to practice for another happy couple's nuptials.

'I couldn't save her, Father. I was too late! I let her die, she died because of me!'

'Now James, that is not true. What would you have done? What could you have done?'

Doctor Dara, louder now, tried to shake his son out of his misery and continued, 'There wasn't a way, James. She was gone. There is nothing – look at me, look at me now, that's better – nothing you could have possibly done to save her! Stop torturing yourself, James. Stop it, stop it!'

The tenor sang on, 'Welcome, welcome, welcome. Welcome, welcome, welcome, Glorious Morn. Nature smiles at thy return ...'

James let his father hold him and the music roll over him until his tears were spent. He didn't know how long they stood there for, but when he looked up again the choir and musicians had gone.

Doctor Dara dried his son's face with his handkerchief, tenderly. Softly, he spoke again, 'James, son, I will try to help you. I know I cannot make up for her loss, but I swear I will try.'

They walked slowly together back up the aisle again to the same pew and sat a little longer.

Eventually James turned to his father. 'Perhaps if I had known more of midwifery and the dangers that can happen during pregnancy I could have saved Marguerite,' he said softly.

Doctor Dara shook his head and sat in silence for a couple of minutes. He savoured a new idea, and then turned to share it with his son. 'James, if that is truly how you feel … well, I know you could not have helped Marguerite, but perhaps you could save other women. In memory, if you like, of her. A dedication. And other children would not have to grow up motherless as Daniel has to.'

James looked at his father, something like a quiet interest in his eyes for the first time since Marguerite's death. His father's heart opened and gladdened at the sight and he warmed to his topic excitedly.

'We both know of doctors who have gone to study the art of midwifery in Paris, James. Laurence Stone mentioned it to you, and you were unsure before, I understand, but now you could embrace the change and the challenge and become a man-midwife. It would be a worthy thing to do, Ryan and other detractors be damned. And you have your French from that summer spent there helping Thomas Lynch with his trading. For Marguerite,' he trailed off.

He took James's hand again – it was warm this time – and looked to his son for his assent. 'It will give you purpose James, help you to heal.'

As they took their leave, Doctor Dara rubbed the lucky stone vigorously and turned to his son as if the action had helped him to remember the message that he was to pass on.

'Son, Marguerite, before she died, asked her mother for a Galway girl to help care for the baby. Two of the O'Flaherty sisters – you know, Liam's girls – are to stay with Sarah Lynch. Your mother kept in contact with the family as you asked. She says that they have grown up to be fine young ladies, and recommended them.

'Their own mother is still a shadow of her former self though, and the four youngest children are being sent to their Aunt Mairin – the herb woman in Barna – as Mrs O'Flaherty cannot cope, poor woman. Mairin has already helped Carissa a great deal, I believe, and has been teaching her about plants and their use in remedies. Apparently the girl shows a great deal of interest and promise.

'Once Carissa and Aileen have adjusted to their new Dublin life, one of the girls will come to your house to live and mind Daniel for you. She will arrive while you are away, if that indeed is what you decide to do, and be well settled in by the time you return from your studies.'

James stood and watched his father disappear into the distance. He wished Marguerite would be waiting for him on his return. But she wouldn't, now or ever again. He stood alone on the street and felt his old friend despair sink its teeth into his soul and he sighed, shoulders slumped.

Then he made his own way home, where perhaps he would hold his baby son for the first time since he delivered him and have some food. And another drink, too, just to help him along.

5

To make a French ice cream
Boil a handful of oranges then strain and beat them and
put in half a dozen ounces of sugar and a pint of cream
and sieve the mixture. Put it into a tin with a top and set
the tin into a tub of ice broken up small. Leave for five
hours and then turn out the frozen mixture.

Quinn Household Recipes and Remedies Book

PARIS, 1740–1741

The early evening sun glinted off the Seine, catching on
the ripples like diamonds, tumbling crystals. James Quinn
stood and looked at the water for a while, then turned and
made his way down a cobbled street in search of something
to eat and drink. He took in the bustle of people all around,
breathing in the life that surrounded him.

Inside the restaurant, patrons sat at every table, bathed
in candlelight, gesticulating to make a point in their
conversation, and the delicious aroma of French cuisine
greeted his nostrils, producing a rumbling from his stomach

that reminded him that he had not eaten for some time. He sat and took it all in, drinking wine steadily and smiling as the glow from the drink suffused him with a sense of well-being.

As his dish of boiled beef and herb stew was placed in front of him, he drained the last of his wine and asked for more.

He wanted bread to go with his dish, but was told by his waiter that there was none available, due to the country-wide famine that had begun with the continual wet weather which made the crops bloom with rot and led to the exorbitant prices for grain.

The waiter shrugged his shoulders and left. James nodded to himself, things were bad at home in Ireland too.

He banished the dark thoughts and settled down to enjoy the rest of his meal, ordering more wine to accompany the new French dessert, ice cream.

It was on unsteady, coltish legs that he made his way back to his lodgings, looking at the moon high above and stumbling as he leant back too much in his admiration of the icy white orb, high in the heavens, stars twinkling around it like tiny fireflies darting around in the velvet inky sky.

In the dark, wood-clad room, he took off his boots and opened the long windows which looked onto the inner courtyard of the building.

He pulled off the rest of his clothes, threw them to the floor and took the tiny gold-framed portrait of Marguerite from his belongings, placing it on the ornate table by his bed so he could see her as he lay down.

'Now, my love,' he slurred to her picture, 'here we are in Paris on a moonlit night.' He traced her curved lips with his little finger, kissed her likeness tenderly and reached down and fumbled around to find one of her letters to him. He settled down to read it, bottle of brandy in hand, stroking the pages that she had touched, casting longing glances at her portrait from time to time.

Galway, 7 November 1736

My dearest, darling James,

I hope that the fine fellows of Dublin are treating you well and that city life and studies will not conspire to keep you away from my side for too much longer. I miss you so, and long to see your dear, darling face.

We are all well here. Mama is most delighted at the thought of all the organising she will do for our wedding. Your mama is often here, and your sister too, while our fathers clap each other on the backs delightedly, smoking and drinking fine wines and brandy in Papa's study. I can hear them now; Peg has told them supper will be ready soon, so I suppose that means I should make haste too.

But I just wanted to say, James, that I am so happy, you have made me so happy I might cry with it. My heart feels so full, I am sure it is beating harder, and I wish you were here to rest your ear on it so you could hear it pounding away merrily in anticipation of our wedding and lives together. And the family that we will have, oh, James, I am so excited!

I remember with such bliss that day when you and I walked down through the Spanish Arch to the great grey wall of Galway with the loose stone that only you and I know about. How many love messages were left behind that stone my sweet?

If the wall could talk, all of Galway might be scandalised!

But, my own darling, none of our heavenly love notes were ever discovered; it is as if the angels themselves were keeping watch over our little pieces of paper sleeping snugly behind the aged stone.

Ah James, when I put my hand into the space behind the stone that day and pulled out the linen pouch you had left there for me to find I swear I did not know what was going on.

And when I took the scarlet ribbon from the pouch and you asked me to keep it always as a love token and wear it on my person on our wedding day, I was sure my heart would burst.

I love every tiny bit of you, my love, your face with its dimples and dusting of light freckles across the nose and cheeks, your kind eyes, unruly hair, your smile. Your arms as they hold me, your warm breath as it touches my hair when you reach down to take me into your arms. The way that everybody loves you, even our bad-tempered cat whom I am sure is pregnant again – so many kittens for one furry little body! The way that you always make me smile and feel loved and safe and cherished. And the way that I love you back, with all my heart and soul.

You made me the happiest person alive that day, James Quinn, and every day is the same now that I know we are to be together forever. I think I must be the luckiest girl on earth.

Mama is calling for me now, supper is ready and I will be chided as if I were five years old for being so love-struck as to come to the table late again. But nobody really minds, James, they know how much we adore each other. I will write more again later, my love.

I am yours forever, my darling, and cannot wait to see you again. My arms long to hold you, but you are not here to touch. I love you, James.

Your own Marguerite.

James tossed and turned in an uneasy sleep.

He stared at the serene face of the Blessed Virgin Mary, a smile lifting her lips for eternity, fixed there by the sculptor.

Masses of flowers covered the bower that the statue was carried on, in every colour under the sun. The faithful sang hymns to celebrate her Feast Day, their slow feet charting the progress of the procession.

He could hear the slow hymns now, too slow. His feet tried to take him closer to the crowd, to the Madonna, but it felt as if he was running on sand. The harder he tried to run, the slower his progress, the heavier his heart had to beat to bring him even the tiniest bit nearer. He was sweating, breathing heavily, desperate in his need to get closer. He reached out his arms to her, getting nowhere.

The Blessed Virgin turned her face to James, just a fraction, and the gentle, benevolent smile that had curled the corners of her mouth turned to a grimace and frown lines marred her wooden forehead.

As James watched, she reached within the folds of her blue cloak and took out his Spanish pocketknife, the one his father had given him. She held it, glinting in her hand.

He looked on open-mouthed, still running to try to get to her, wondering what she was going to do with it. 'No!' he shouted. 'Help her!' But the crowd of the faithful did not hear him.

He looked to her again, and saw the swell of her pregnancy under her white gown. She looked near her time. The thought spurred him on and he ran fast again but somehow got even slower, and started to fall to the ground, panting.

The singing became louder, discordant, and the Madonna fixed James with a fraught stare. As the jarring hymns hurt his ears and his heart felt like it might crumble in his chest, crimson blood burst from between her legs, staining her gown and cloak and the masses of flowers that covered the bower that she was carried on, no longer every colour under the sun, just a furious, uniform red.

She raised James's knife to the sky, and brought it down in a swift motion, cutting open her own belly.

Blood and bowel burst through her ragged wound, and James hid his face in his hands as he lay on the ground, curled up to protect himself. The Blessed Virgin cried out to the heavens which mocked her with their silence as her trembling, fumbling hands searched her person and the bower under her frantically.

'My baby! Where is my baby?'

James had not slept much the remainder of that night.

He sat bleary eyed and ill in his bed in the pale morning light and urged himself to rise and start the day. The empty brandy bottle had rolled over and knocked Marguerite's portrait to the ground. He picked the picture up gently, hands trembling as he stroked her face, and left the room in search of coffee.

Having forced down the steaming, murky drink, he left his lodgings. A blast of cool air hit him in the face and punishing rain helped to further waken him. He knew he needed a shave and a long wash, but all his intentions of making a good first impression lay in the dregs of an empty bottle.

James arrived at the Hotel Dieu just as the rain had petered out and seven fellow students turned up, their faces eager and expectant at what was to come. He felt wretched beside them, but smiled and walked with them through the portals of the renowned hospital to the tiered lecture theatre where they had been instructed to go.

A great, dark-haired, elegantly dressed bear of a man took James's arm as he stumbled. James looked up and saw the beaming face and upraised eyebrows over brown twinkling eyes of one who was to become his friend.

'A late night?' asked the bear.

'Too late,' he grimaced and held out his hand to the man. 'James, James Quinn. Pleased to meet you.'

'And I am Andre, Andre Moreau. I think we shall have some fun, you and I, Mr Quinn.'

Their conversation was stopped abruptly as the tutor man-midwives Gregoire the Elder and his son Gregoire the Younger arrived. The Elder stood tall and erect, a shock of white hair out of place with his black bushy eyebrows. The Younger looked like his father must have done twenty years ago.

Gregoire the Elder looked around at his students. 'So, here you learn your craft. You watch how to perform the art of midwifery.' He stopped and lit the pipe that they were to discover rarely left the side of his mouth. 'And you dissect to learn what went wrong and should never go wrong again. Now, follow me, and keep up – to your feet!'

The students struggled to hang on to his every word as the Elder walked briskly along the corridors of the hospital, whose walls were adorned with portraits of famous French physicians and surgeons, pipe smoke trailing him sweet and rich, the Younger bringing up the rear as though they were troublesome ducklings being kept in check by their duck and drake.

'Our hospital was founded by Archbishop Saint-Landry in 651 and has continued to grow since that time. We are a charity hospital that offers our services free to the poor sick of Paris. Many walk straight in, having been next door to Mass at Notre Dame. We boast a large staff of attending physicians and surgeons,' he paused and stopped walking. 'Hello ladies, make sure to get back to bed and rest now,' he greeted two women trying to support each other and keeping close to the wall.

One was heavily pregnant and walked with a waddling gait, while the second had obviously given birth recently, as James noticed that the front of her gown was soaking wet.

Her milk had come on, and as they passed he got a nutty-sweet aroma.

The Elder continued his walkabout at a pace, stopping now and again to greet people and take great mouthfuls of pipe smoke.

'Under our roof lies La Charité, a special ward for women in childbirth. They are attended to by the holy sisters and trained midwives. Some two hundred years ago, a number of our surgeons began a new tradition – they studied the art of midwifery and so became *chirurgen accoucheurs*, man-midwives. They are called upon for difficult cases in La Charité. Hello sisters,' he bowed to five nuns, chattering like the magpies whose colour they sported, as they pushed a food cart. The earthy aroma of boiled cabbage hit James's nose and his stomach rolled over.

He covered his mouth and stopped for a moment but when he looked up he realised that the rest of the students had moved on and Gregoire the Younger was looking at him sternly.

'You are aware that, over the years, when midwives were unable to complete a delivery, or if other complications arose, a physician was called upon. He prescribed the lancet or scarification or leeches to promote bleeding. He ordered medicines to regulate the imbalance in the woman's humours. Some remedies were so vile the physician was forced to prescribe them by enema. And then, of course, when these treatments did not work, we, the surgeon man-midwives, were called to the birth chamber to complete the delivery by use of our hands and instruments.'

The Elder stopped and faced his students. 'At those desperate times the mothers and infants in their wombs were in grave circumstances, close to life's end.

'Oftentimes the infant was already dead but not born. We came upon desperate difficulties in those birth chambers and were forced to carry out cruel procedures to save the life of the mother. Sometimes, and against all hope, we brought a living infant into the world. We have an unfair reputation, my friends: the last call, the last choice, the uncertain outcomes.'

As if to emphasise his point, a porter pushed a trolley past them, bearing the body of a dead woman, wrapped in blood-soaked sheets. The Elder walked on.

He motioned towards a large, ornately framed portrait, 'and so, we have the most famous of all French midwives, Louise Bourgeois. She was the royal midwife to Queen Marie de Medicis in the early seventeenth century, her book is part of your essential reading.

'But, Louise Bourgeois was strongly opposed to the presence of medical men in the lying-in room, although from time to time she did consult with surgeons. In one difficult case mentioned in her book, she insisted that the surgeon be hidden from view by placing the bed curtain between him and the poor labouring woman. Otherwise Louise was afraid the woman would die of dread and shame due to her violated modesty.'

He walked on and gestured to another painting, 'Now we see the great man-midwife Francois Mauriceau. He wrote that men were called to assist at childbirth after days of unsuccessful labour. The child was likely dead, and the life of the mother almost over. Yet the surgeon man-midwife who delivered the child was treated like a butcher and a hangman. See the way the artist has highlighted his hands with a beam of light from above? These hands move the infant from the darkness of the womb into the light of the world. But enough of art and history, we are here to tend to the living,' and so saying, he strode on again, calling over his shoulder, 'let us return to our lecture room. We will discuss the books you must analyse and learn. We will instruct you about your duties. And we will tell you what we expect of you in one word! Magnificence. That is all we will accept. Anything else is failure.'

6

How to make rose water

Fill half a pot with fresh water. Gather up an armful of
roses and pick the petals from them and put them into
the water. Place the pot on the fire and let it boil, then
take it off and let it cool before pouring the rose water
into glass bottles with stoppers. Dab the rose water on
your wrists and sides of your neck for a long-lasting
fragrance.

Quinn Household Recipes and Remedies Book

Gregoire the Younger took his charges to a nearby coffee
house at the end of their seemingly never-ending day.
He smiled to himself at their tired silence as they left the
hospital and walked along the banks of the Seine.

'So,' he said, 'we will come to this quiet chamber,' he
paused and gestured around the upper salon of the coffee
house, 'at the end of every week to discuss your progress.
Remember that in this place we are all equal. But I am
more equal,' he smiled impishly at them.

'In this room we can address your weaknesses. I can lash
you with my tongue where nobody can hear. Sometimes
I may praise you, but not too often. The same strictures

applied to me and to my father before me. Tonight you will begin to study the texts that describe the anatomy of woman with child. Now, James, tell me of your anatomy course in Ireland,' Gregoire the Younger said, jolting him from a sleepy, yawning reverie.

James squirmed in his seat, ashamed at having been caught out. He blushed. 'Well,' he cleared his throat and continued, 'at Trinity College in Dublin, where I studied, the bodies and body parts were all male. They were steeped in wine to preserve them but they became discoloured and foul after a time.' He paused and looked at his tutor and fellow students, 'I have never dissected any woman, pregnant or not, as none were available.'

Gregoire interrupted him with an imperious wave of the hand. 'Yes, yes, that is the same story I hear every time we begin a new course. But we will change that very quickly. At first you will study the theory of the female anatomy from your texts. Within the month each of you will assist at the frequent post-mortems in La Charité. Soon afterwards, each of you will be responsible in turn for dissecting those mothers who die.

'Now, my blessings to you, *adieu* until morning comes. James, my friend, may I walk with you?'

James's heart sank as he was sure he was in for a stern talking to for daydreaming during lectures. He nodded his consent even though he longed for escape.

As they sat on an uncomfortable bench and watched the river's progress through the city, Gregoire turned to James.

'This morning, James, you looked ill, pale, your hands trembled. You have come to us to learn about the most venerable thing you may ever be taught in your whole life, yet you arrive untidy and unshaven.' He stopped and looked at the water.

'But the most unforgivable thing, most unacceptable thing, is the foul stench of brandy on your breath. It is intolerable to me, my father, the women of Paris, any woman for that matter.'

James started to speak, to excuse himself, but Gregoire held up his hand to silence him.

'We do not need to know your problems, James.' He softened his tone, angry light leaving his eyes, and went on. 'However, we know that you must have a good heart for there are few men who wish to take on the difficult and contentious life of the man-midwife. We are no different to those who went before us. We must learn from their experience. My father and I have a gift for you to read.'

So saying, Gregoire passed a book to James who turned it over in his hands.

'When you return to your lodgings read the part I have marked,' he said and then looked him directly in the eye again, 'and James, no more brandy or wine for you, my friend. The next time we might not be so forgiving.' And with those words he strolled off into the evening.

Andre came upon James still sitting on the same bench looking forlornly at the river, flipping the pages of Mauriceau's text.

'That bad?' he asked.

'That bad,' replied James.

'Ah, Mauriceau's "Conditions necessary for a man-midwife ... Above all, he must be sober, no tipler that so at all times he may have his wits about him",' quoted Andre.

James looked up at him in amazement and the French man shrugged off his knowledge.

'Let us walk, James, and you can tell me why you drink, for you can't hide the condition.'

James flushed under Andre's scrutiny.

'"He must be pitiful, patient and compassionate",' he continued. 'Maybe I come to the root of your problem, my friend. "He ought to have a pleasant countenance, and to be as neat in his clothes as in his person, that the poor women who have need of him, be not affrightened at him. He must be healthful, strong and robust; because this is the most laborious and painful of all the workings of surgery." Well James, what would Mauriceau say about you? Do not let this man anywhere near a pregnant or labouring woman until he has shaved, bathed, and had a change of clothes.'

Andre paused as he realised his words had struck home with his companion, who looked like a little boy who had been caught doing something he ought not to, downcast and penitent.

He clapped James on the shoulder.

'But James, would I meet Mauriceau's strong standards? I think not! He continues to say: '"Above all he should have small hands, for the easier introduction of them into the womb; yet strong with the fingers long, especially the fore-finger, the better to reach and touch the inner orifice. He must have no rings on his fingers, and his nails well pared, when he goes about his work, for fear of hurting the womb."'

Both men stopped and Andre guffawed as he held his large hands out for James's inspection.

'I need a friend, even if the one that has come has hands more akin to shovels,' said James.

Andre beamed at him. 'Consider me still your friend, even after such a grievous insult.'

James Quinn felt absurdly nervous as he stood on the steps outside the impressive door of the large house on the Left

Bank. The building was brightly lit from the inside, casting a soft glow onto the dark street.

His first month of study was over, and he couldn't have done it without Andre's help. The Frenchman helped him while James's mind craved brandy to shut out the pain from his body and soul as he mourned Marguerite, clear-headed for the first time since her death. The punishing, painful time was added to by a heavy schedule and night calls, and from now on he would be expected to carry out full duties competently. Which was why he was here tonight.

He had realised, reading from the book that had been given to him at the end of that tough, hungover first day of his new Parisian life, that he needed to be able to capably examine a living, breathing woman. Nobody he spoke to of it wanted to entertain the idea, and he had no help, but insistent asking around the better streets of the city in blackest night had whispered the same answer to him again and again.

And so, here he stood, heart hammering, palms sweating, trying to breathe deeply to calm down. He thought of Marguerite, wondered what she would think of what he was about to do. Whether she would forgive him. For though he had slept with his wife, it had always been done out of love and in the darkness rather than in any pursuit of medical knowledge of the workings of the female body.

He sent up a little prayer to her in Heaven, bowing his head. 'Forgive me, my love.'

It was too late to back out now, even if what had seemed such a great idea in the light of day did not seem so great now, as he stood alone in the inky night.

He raised his hand to the great brass knocker again before his courage deserted him entirely, hugging the bag that he had brought tight to his chest as if to gain some comfort from it, and the door opened. A servant stood there before him in burgundy livery.

He ushered James in through the long hallway with many gold-scrolled mirrors hung on the walls intensifying the candlelight, through to a waiting room where a couple of other men sat too large on ornate chairs. As he took in the opulence of the room and the dark blue velvet curtains that cut out the night, one of the men tried to make conversation, asking him which of Madam's girls he would be visiting tonight and recommending a couple to him with a lewd wink.

James got to his feet to leave, sure now that he had made a mistake, but just then the door opened and the servant reappeared to say, 'Madam will see you now.'

He followed the servant to another room, cosy, but just as lushly furnished. The tall, graceful woman rose from her desk and laid her spectacles on top of the papers she had been going through. She ran her hand down her silk skirts to smooth them before presenting a perfectly manicured, many ringed hand to James to kiss.

'Madam,' he said, touching his lips to her perfumed flesh. She wore rose water, just like his mother, but it did not endear her to him any.

'Well,' she replied, 'you are not one of our regular gentlemen, and as such I like to meet and talk to new visitors to my house to better gain an appreciation of what it is that they are looking for.'

She paused and smiled, looking at him intently, sizing him up. 'I would say a young girl, maybe not so city smart, kind and accommodating for you – I have just the girl in mind.'

James stared at the beauty spot above her lip as she spoke, and he took a deep breath as he knew now was the time to lay out his needs to the businesswoman who stood before him.

'Madam, I have some special requirements,' he started, as she cut across his conversation.

'Ah,' she said, 'I am usually a better judge of character. You prefer something a little more, shall we say, out of the ordinary? You like to be, perhaps, tied up with delicious silken bonds? Treated as a boy who likes to be spanked? Watch a couple of my beautiful girls delight each other?'

He blushed furiously as her list went on, and cleared his throat to speak again. 'No, nothing like that,' he said, shaking his head in emphasis.

She looked at him curiously this time, crinkling her eyes in question, and waved her hand imperiously for him to go on.

'She must be clean,' he said.

Madam looked affronted, and with a sharp 'tsk' escaping her compressed lips answered him, 'My girls are so clean you could, and can, should you so desire, eat a meal off them.'

'No clap,' he continued, counting on his fingers.

'Sir! This is a superior establishment, as many gentlemen will attest to! We wish to treat you to supreme rapture rather than a dose of supreme annoyance!'

'No lues venerea, no whore's pox,' James continued, another finger poised mid-air.

'We do not sell the fiery material and the hot piss of the citadel in danger. You may engage in armour when entering the covered way, should you wish!' she continued, breathing heavily.

He put a hand out as if to calm her. 'I will need candles,' he said gently.

'Well, monsieur, then there will be more money for me. Doubtless this maiden should be young, comely and willing.' The Madam paused, head to one side as she waited for him to continue.

'I want to know her completely; I want to know her body.'

'What of her mind?'

James shrugged his shoulders.

'Come back in three nights' time, monsieur. I will have a fresh young whore for you then. But now we will talk of price.'

7

A cordial water to strengthen the nerves
Take two large handfuls of lavender and add to fresh water in a pot. Put the pot on the fire and boil the mixture until steam rises from it, pour it out and leave to cool. Once it is cooled add a large spoonful of honey, mix well and then take a small glass at any time as required.

Quinn Household Recipes and Remedies Book

James stood in the middle of the bedchamber as Madam ushered the young blonde woman over to him.

'This is Avril. Now you may curtsy to your benefactor, my dear,' and so saying, she left the room, closing the door softly behind her.

Avril stood in front of him, nervous, and glorious in her youthful good health. Her blue eyes were bright, her mouth curved like a small red bow, light hair shone. Her gown was obviously borrowed, for it seemed as if she was ill at ease in its magnificent folds, the profusion of lace at the cuffs and indecently low bust.

James led her to the bedside, gently taking her by the hand.

He lit the candles slowly and placed a jar of lubricating pomade by the bed as she looked on apprehensively.

In the adjoining room, the unseen eyes of other whores peeped through a spy hole. They were all intrigued by the new gentleman who had requested the most unusual requirements.

'Do not be afraid. I mean you no harm,' James said to her, taking her chin softly in his hand and turning her face to his.

'Talk to me, for I am scared,' she whispered.

'Look at me. Have no fear, I will treat you well,' he said, appraising her.

'You have eyes of such delicate blue colour. See this part,' he pointed to his own eye for emphasis, 'this is the iris. The ancients called it after the great goddess of rainbow, sea and sky whose golden wings carried her with her messages between gods and mortals.'

He traced a finger gently around her mouth. 'And here the labia oris, those lips that pout with their sweet vermilion borders, there the philtrum, the love groove that inflamed carnal desire in ancient Greece.'

Avril breathed softly.

'It is also said that God sends an angel to the womb to teach each baby the wisdom and the wonders of Heaven and Earth. Then, just as the baby enters the world, the angel says "shush" and touches the lip to make the baby forget. Some say that it is God himself who leaves the indent of his finger, just here,' he touched the groove that ran from the bottom of her nose to the top of her lip.

The whores listened on intently, safe in their dark room, taking turns in watching the man with the kindly way, perhaps a little heartsore and jealous that no one had thought to treat any of them thus, as they giggled and jostled past.

James ran his fingers down Avril's throat to her collar bone.

'And this,' he continued, 'this long firm bone is called the clavicle, the key, as it unlocks the secrets of the shoulder to help it move.'

He turned Avril around and gently eased the gown down from her shoulders. As he ran his hands along her back, recalling the bones and muscles that support it, she shivered at his touch.

'You must speak,' she said.

James's fingers traced the twin hollows on her lower back.

'And these, the dimples of Venus, where Vulcan, the god of fire, touched the goddess's body in a lover's embrace. Thereafter, at each tryst he poured honey in them then sipped the amber fluid.

'Between the love dimples, the os sacrum, the sacred bone, sacred because it was thought to carry the precious male essence from the spine to the yard and deep into the matrix. And so to here, in the cleft, the coccyx bone or cuckoo bird, because it looks like a cuckoo's beak.'

Madam's eye widened at the scene before her through the spy hole. One of her girls had urged her to come and see what was transpiring in the bedchamber. She drew her breath in sharply as she watched James run his hands along Avril's naked back, the girl holding the rest of her dress in front of her breasts as the examination of her body went on.

In the room that held so much fascination to the other women of the house, James turned Avril to him and helped her out of the rest of her clothes as she blushed and kept her eyes downcast.

He laid her slowly, gently, on the bed and looked at her. She touched his hand for reassurance and he smiled before continuing to speak.

'So, to the via lactea, the milky way, the secret valley, bound on each side by those soft mounds topped by rosebuds. Their petals open to the touch of lips, the mammae that nurture the world.

'One day you may feed a baby born of love. Many authors write of the best paps and teats. These writers say that the breasts should be of medium size, soft and unwrinkled, to receive and concoct there a sufficient quantity of milk.

'They must be found free from the scars of former impostumes, the breasts must be firm and fleshy so that their vital heat may be stronger. As to the nipples, they must be well shaped, not too big nor too hard, nor sunk in too deep; but they must be a little raised, of a moderate bigness and firmness.'

James touched Avril below her left breast. 'And this, this mark is called a witch's teat.'

She shivered.

His hands moved down to her navel. 'Thy navel is like a round goblet which wants not liquor, or so it says in the good book.'

She started to squirm away a little as James moved his eyes further down her body, and he placed a gentle hand on her thigh.

'The omphalos of Greece, umbilicus of Rome, the centre to which was attached the funis, the navel-string, the cord, from here it is said there is total access to the underworld.'

So saying, he put his finger into her navel and tickled her there.

Madam had seen enough, and beckoning her girls to follow she left her hiding place and rushed in to the bedchamber, where she came upon a twisting, squealing Avril, flushed and breathing heavily on the bed.

She pulled James up sharply from his seat on the bed in a flurry of damask and feminine outrage. 'Shame, shame on you, enough of your strangeness for now!' she said, and all but pushed him out of the door.

'Madam, I meant no harm, and she has not been harmed. I must come back to see Avril again,' he implored, stumbling as he tried to find his feet.

She sniffed disdainfully; money was money after all.

'So be it,' she answered stiffly. 'Until the next time then.'

'This was a dreadful week of sorrows, of sickness and disease. Many mothers in St Joseph's ward have died of inflammation of the womb,' said Gregoire the Elder as he addressed his students, sadness written heavy across his face, plain for all to see.

'At first there was the joy of birth and the newborns but then the devastation of the mothers' departure from this life. We worked diligently to save the poor wretches but to no avail. Now we pray the terrible scourge will soon take its leave of our hospital. On the sad morning before us, and halfway through your time with us to learn how to become man-midwives, we must dissect five more women who left this valley of tears only yesterday to seek peace in the arms of the Saviour,' he paused. 'James, we will take your case study to start with.'

'Marie Thérèse Renaud was twenty years of age, the wife of a candle-maker, delivered of her first baby last Tuesday,' James started to relate the details of his patient.

'Three days after the birth she felt a great heaviness in the bottom of her belly. She became swelled and blown up almost as big as before delivery. There was pain and discomfort making water and going to the stool. She had a great fever with difficulty breathing, hiccups and vomiting.'

'And what of the lochia?' asked his tutor.

'Marie Thérèse had suppression of discharge from the fourth day,' he answered.

'Ah, the worst and most dangerous symptom that can befall a woman after delivery,' said Gregoire the Elder, shaking his white head. 'Continue.'

'When the inflammation was perceived the cure of it was sought. The privvy parts were anointed with warm oil and an attempt was made to extract any such corrupt things as may remain in the womb after delivery.

'The heat of the humours was tempered by a cooling diet of broth of pullet, not too strong of the flesh, with the cooling herbs, lettuce, purslane and borage. A drink concocted of the roots of succory, dogs-grass, barley and liquorice was administered, and a little syrup of maiden-hair.'

'Which treatments were prescribed?' asked the Elder.

'Anodyne enemas were used to draw the lochia downwards. A decoction of camomile, mallows, asparagus and linseed was laid on the lower parts – the same recipe was also placed into the womb.

'A very hot plaster with oil of lilies and hogs grease was placed on the lower belly. The thighs were bathed and rubbed downwards with an emollient decoction; cupping glasses were likewise applied to the inside of her thighs.'

'Was she blooded in the foot?' came the next enquiry from his teacher.

'No, the redundant humours were bled from the arm as bleeding from the foot could increase the inflammation of the womb.'

'Your regimen was most favourable, James,' said Gregoire.

'The fever had too great a hold on her. During the convulsions we prayed for her but death took her away. My heart was heavy for I was attached to her. Her infant girl is baptised Maria by the midwives, who also sorrow,' James passed the information on sadly.

'James, my son awaits you for the dissections. We will discuss Marie Thérèse with the other cases. Be about your business,' and Gregoire put a heavy, reassuring hand on his shoulder as he left the room.

James entered the quiet side room where post-mortems were carried out, eyes flitting quickly over the bodies that lay on tables covered with once-white sheets which were now stained with so much life blood. It broke his heart, and he sighed from deep inside.

The room smelled of death and putrefaction. James resisted the urge to cover his nose with his hand, wishing he had a posy to mask the odour.

Gregoire the Younger noticed his arrival and said, 'Join me, James, for the dissection of Marie Thérèse, then we will work separately. I will keep the notes as required by the hospital board. We must be truthful and report fully any misadventure by the midwives, by ourselves or by the patient. Look most carefully to discover any putrefaction and its cause.'

James nodded and slipped back the sheet to reveal the young woman's body whose face and parts he knew so well of late.

As he reached for the shining knife the saliva dried in his mouth, and he felt an unseen hand grip him by the throat. He could not take a proper breath.

He could hear his heart thumping, hurting his chest. He took tiny, quick sucks at the air. He felt his hands tingling and shaking as he could not get enough of it into his lungs.

He was much panicked. His legs shook and felt like they would support his weight no longer. His vision was covered with large black swimming shapes. He was overcome with an impending sense of doom; he was surely about to die. His heart must stop under the strain. He had to run, to escape, but he couldn't move. As if from a great distance, down a hollow tunnel, he could hear Gregoire's anxious voice.

James dropped the knife; it clattered to the ground noisily as he held on to the table for dear life, panting and shaking.

Gregoire ran to him and threw his arms around him, holding him tightly as James trembled and shuddered uncontrollably.

He cried out in distress, but still Gregoire held strong as the dread overtook James. The men sank slowly to the floor as one, and tutor cradled student, rocking him gently. James desperately wanted a drink, to feel the warming liquid slide down the back of his throat and numb his feelings.

When the storm had passed, James disentangled himself from his teacher and, looking him in the eyes all the time, told him of Marguerite's tale and the death of his heart. He told him of his terrible nights and daytime fears, and Gregoire the Younger listened intently throughout.

His father, unseen at the door of the room, roused by the commotion, also listened in. When James quietened, he beckoned his son over to him.

They talked quietly as their student still sat on the floor, motionless and quietly staring at nothing at all. The Elder left the room briefly and returned carrying a small book.

'James,' said Gregoire the Elder softly, crouching down to place his hand on his student's shoulder for the second time that day, 'we are all touched by adversity and those who are gifted by God with tender deep emotions feel the hurt so much more. But with time the pain that aches in our hearts will lessen. And so I read to you to remind you of Francois Mauriceau's tragedy. He wrote: "About three years since, one of my sisters, not yet one and twenty years of age, being about eight and a half months gone with her fifth child, was suddenly surprised with strong frequent pains and floodings."

'The midwife sent for a surgeon to advise on the case. He chose to retire from the birth chamber without assisting but advised "to give her all the sacraments as nothing can be done for her". The midwives summoned Mauriceau who rushed to his sister's side. "I saw as soon as I came in so pitiful a spectacle that all the passions of my soul were at that instant agitated with many and different commotions".'

Gregoire the Elder shifted into a more comfortable position and continued, 'His sister had lost more than three quarts of blood and grew ever weaker. With very great difficulty Mauriceau was able to deliver the child and placenta. His dear sister retained perfect senses but she and the newborn were dead within the hour.

'Yet Mauriceau, who was overcome by sadness, became the best loved of all man-midwives in France. And he wrote his story so that those with tender hearts would take courage.

'Now, James, come, for the spirits of Marie Thérèse and Francois Mauriceau, the souls of all the women and infants that you are yet to save, and we Gregoires, we will all aid you.'

The men helped James to his feet. Gregoire the Younger looked at him, and handed him the knife that had fallen to the floor.

'James,' he said softly, 'you should talk more about this – your burden is too terrible for one man alone to carry. Share and be supported.' He squeezed James's shoulder with his free hand.

And as James accepted the knife, his tutors smiled at each other and Gregoire the Elder said, 'Good. Good. All is as it should be, James.'

8

To take away freckles

Take four large spoonfuls of elderflower water and put it in a bowl with one large spoonful of oil of tartar that is in liquid form. Mix well together. Wash the face with this as often as liked and leave it on to dry.

Quinn Household Recipes and Remedies Book

'Madam saw me from her carriage. I was sitting on the ground as the rain poured down. She said she saw my potential through the downpour and the dirt and grime that covered me. She told me to hold my skirts away from the seat in the carriage; they were covered with horse dung.' Avril answered James's question as to how she came to be at Madam's establishment, though it hurt in the telling.

He looked at her intently as she lay on the bed, her creamy nakedness covered by a sheet, the flickering light turning the silken grey material into a rippling pool.

'I came from the Low Countries to France. I am from a very small village that you never would have heard of. I doubt that you would find it on a map. Its name is not important anyway, and I will never go there again.

'My family, the Hansens, had a small farm. We worked very hard but we were happy. And then a great sickness came and stole my parents, brothers and sister and left me alone in the world. Well, I had an uncle who took me in. But he wanted to use me in a way that I didn't want so I ran away and found myself in Paris, and here I am. My mother was French,' a lone tear slid down her cheek and James wiped it away gently.

'But that was then and this is now,' she recovered swiftly, brushing away James's concern and sympathy. 'Madam has been kind, some of the girls less so as they know I will be sold for a high price because I am not experienced in love-making. They are afraid I will steal their custom away, but they should not be,' she blushed.

'You must talk to me,' she said briskly, taking charge, re-enacting what had gone on the last time he visited. She felt so emboldened that she placed his hand on her navel, and pushed down the sheet.

His hand crept down the pale skin of her torso, slowly, softly.

From behind the spy hole came furious whispering, 'What's he saying now?' followed by a yelp as a foot was trodden on and, 'shh, come closer.'

'The mons pubis, the mound of Venus,' said James, 'the great doubling of the skin, the volvo or wrapper of the ancients, the vulva, the cleft of Venus.'

'What perversion is this? Why must he talk so much?' demanded the whore who at present had her eye so close to the spy hole it may as well have been stuck into place with glue.

'There the nymphae, the veiled brides, those female spirits of spring and grove with acorn or myrtle berry in full bloom,' he said quietly.

'Fetch Madam, quickly,' hissed the whore.

'And so,' he continued, 'Bacchus, the god of revelry, and Aphrodite, the Greek Venus, gave birth to the god of marriage. Through the ages happy couples sing their hymns of love to Hymenaeus, the guardian of the Cyprian strait, the sanctum muliebre, Cupid's cloister, Heaven's gate.'

'Hush now and be about your businesses,' whispered Madam furiously as she moved past her girls roughly to get to the spy hole. She settled in to watch.

James went on. 'And so, the part the Latins called the sword scabbard, resting place for the yard and the aura seminis, here the hysteros, the matricis and its neck the os tincae, it feels like a puppy's snout; in childbirth, the midwives' garland.'

He stopped. Avril looked up at him from behind the curtain of her hair, and swept it aside so that her tresses lay over her shoulder. She regarded him intently under the soft glow of the candlelight and the unseen stare of her Madam.

James Quinn sat in the lecture hall awaiting the arrival of Gregoire the Elder. All around him his fellow students chattered. He didn't feel like joining in this morning, and though a few sentences had been thrown his way he showed his disinterest at joining in by holding up his textbook and smiling ruefully.

Suddenly James wasn't sitting in the lecture room any more. He found himself retracing his steps, up the stairs to the bedchamber where he found the women weeping and his one true love lying on the bed undelivered, bloody, made mute by death.

He heard her weak calls in his head, pleading for help, even though he had not been there to listen to them at the time. They reverberated in his skull and he put his hands over his ears to try to shut the pitiful cries out.

When he took his hands away again he looked at them in disbelief, turning them one way and then the other. They were covered in her blood, painted red, then rust, and now crimson.

He blinked to clear his vision, and sure enough he was still sitting in the lecture room, textbook fallen to the floor and forgotten. He bent to pick it up, all the while thinking on sin and how it was impossible for one person sitting on high in Heaven to decide that his Marguerite deserved to suffer for her supposed wrongdoings.

But then, He allowed His own to suffer torments on the wooden, splintered cross that day under the relentless Golgotha sun. Outside the gates of the city of Jerusalem, so His dead son's poor broken body could not contaminate the living. A law made by men, enacted by God. James shook his head in wonder.

He allowed the painful memories of Marguerite's last day to take his breath away once again and cover his shoulders with their desperate mantle. His sorrowful reverie was disturbed as his tutor entered and clapped his hands together once to bring his class to attention.

'Yesterday we learned about natural labour, to wit, that it be at full time, that it be speedy and without any ill accident, and that the child be alive. We considered the condition of the mother and child and how an expert midwife conducts the labour and delivery. Our Mr Moreau was able, as usual, to quote from texts from memory. Well done Andre, perhaps you will now give others a chance to shine. Today we will learn of difficult labours. Did you study your texts in preparation? Good. Now kindly pay attention to my son.'

Gregoire the Younger stood in front of the table in the hushed lecture room, instrument raised above his head, arms outstretched.

The long steel rod with its sharp hook sliced through the air then bit deeply into the wood as it swung in its downward arc.

James flinched and he noticed his fellow students do the same.

Hauling on its ebony handle, the Younger pulled hard and the table moved towards him, grating across the floor. He released the hook with difficulty then held it aloft again.

'This, my friends, is the crotchet. Andre, there are some here, please pass them along. As you know, the crotchet is used to thrust into and hook a dead foetus to aid in its extraction from the womb,' continued Gregoire. 'We know the baby is dead when the mother has felt no movement for some time, putrid fluid leaks from the womb, and the infant's head has collapsed and is soft. Midwives only use their hands to conduct delivery, so it falls on surgeons and man-midwives to use this destructor. Pity the days you have to use it.'

He showed how the crotchet was used to hook into the head, eye socket or other parts of the foetus within reach, and how using all his strength the man-midwife would drag the tiny dead unborn into the world, a bloody mess rather than a pink living infant to be handed into its mother's arms.

'But enough,' he continued. 'We have had enough of death and destruction. For we have our successes too, we bring infants alive to their mothers who cry out with joy in that first embrace.

'We employ these next methods when the delivery is imminent but delayed, and the mother in much distress.

Consider here the fillet, or loop as others call it. In ancient times, Hippocrates knew of this method to extract living infants from the womb once the neck of the matrix was open. The Ancients used loops of silk or leather. Now we avail of horsehair, whalebone, or cane mounted in wood or metal handles. And now behold,' the Younger paused and with a great sense of ceremony unveiled a set of instruments that lay on the table beside him.

'See here the *main de fer*, the iron hands, the delivery forceps first shown in this city only twenty years ago. These versions are cumbersome and can slip off, but with some improvement, the forceps will be of great use in man-midwifery during difficult births. We wait in great expectation of the day.'

'Thank you,' said Gregoire the Elder to his son. 'Now we will make a demonstration. Ah James, yes, come and join me.'

James left his seat and walked on to join his teacher.

'So far we have persuaded the mother and her onlookers of the impossibility of being delivered without help. Thus resolved, we must place her across the bed. Here James, up, up onto the table and help me to demonstrate, assistance from among you, please.'

With help from a few students, Gregoire readied James as if for delivery and spoke, 'She must lie on her back, her hips raised a little higher than her head. She must fold her legs so as her heels be towards her buttocks, and her thighs spread, and held so by a couple of strong persons.

'Likewise, others hold her arms. The sheet must cover her thighs for decency, here like this,' and he pulled the sheet that was there for the purpose over James, fixing it so it laid flat and just so.

'The woman so fixed is constrained as on the rack,' Gregoire continued. 'Let the man-midwife then anoint the womb with oil or fresh butter. So James, try to escape the clutches of your husband and family.'

James struggled to no avail and Gregoire looked down at him, a wicked glint in his eye.

'Now we recall the ceremony of the Hebrews, when the child becomes a man,' Gregoire paused for dramatic effect. 'In France we call it "the cut" – circumcision, friend James.'

Gregoire pulled up his sleeves and then threw a knife and scissors between James's outstretched thighs.

As the instruments clattered on the wooden table, the student assistants gripped James tightly while he panicked and cried out, lashing with his fists at those nearest to him. Gregoire reached forward and then paused, looking down at the struggling man.

'Thank you, James. Now perhaps you have felt like a mother in desperation, if only for a moment.'

The sun shone down on the two men as they made their way down the broad, leafy streets of St Germain. James and Andre were in search of a coffee house that fine Sunday.

'James, my friend, did you see the new midwife at the Hotel Dieu? My, what a veritable beauty! Her lush little behind could fit just perfectly in my manly paw,' Andre smiled and gave him a playful shove as their laughter rang out.

'Ah, and now I smell another bewitching aroma. In here we shall go, for I declare the quality of that coffee to be excellent, even though I have not yet tasted it.' James smiled at his friend, who considered himself quite the expert in food, drink and, of course, women.

As they sat, Andre looked around and spied three glamorous young ladies. He blessed the gods again; luck was always with him when it came to finding entrancing members of the opposite sex. He tugged on James's sleeve, 'See there, James, sent from Heaven just for us. I will take the angel, the little blonde, and you *mon ami* can have the other two.'

And smiling he left the table and went to introduce himself. James recognised the women from the brothel. He lifted his coffee cup in salute, smiling, and put a finger to his lips as if to tell the ladies not to say a word.

Andre called James over to join them. His many charms had not worked on the angel, who appeared to have eyes only for his long-limbed friend, but he didn't mind unduly as her companions were taken with him, and two were always better than one.

'James, say something romantic to your beautiful lady friend,' said Andre, playfully digging him in the ribs as the table's occupants erupted with laughter.

Avril blushed becomingly and twisted in her seat a little.

James smiled and touched her hand in understanding. He thought she looked lovely today, with her hair all caught up at the back and ringlets falling over her ears. She wore a fine, emerald-coloured gown, embroidered with lighter green leaves and flowers intertwining. Her modesty panel matched the dress perfectly and had a becoming froth of cream lace at the top.

'*Cailín deas ailinn atá tú,*' he said softly to her.

'Well friend, what is this strange tongue you address the French race with?' enquired Andre, clutching at his heart in mock horror.

James smiled, 'Irish, the language of my home.'

'So tell her again, James.'

'*Cailín deas ailinn atá tú*,' even softer this time. James looked Avril deep in the eyes. 'You are a beautiful girl.'

'James, my friend, I can tell you have a great way with women. Give us more of your sayings or tell a tale from Ireland,' chuckled Andre, looking at their female companions.

'I'm not a storyteller,' James replied.

'Tell us something romantic then,' begged Clara, one of the other girls.

'Well,' he said, 'have you heard of Diarmuid?'

The blank faces around the table confirmed that they had not.

'He had a love spot.'

'A love spot?' asked Andre.

'A love spot,' replied James as giggles circled the table.

'More, more, tell us more!' demanded Andre, slapping his thigh.

'It was on his forehead.'

'His forehead, you say, surely not there. Perhaps he was a unicorn, or had freckles,' Andre led a fresh bout of laughter which grew in volume and ribald tone.

James continued, 'Diarmuid had a love spot on his forehead. If any woman saw the love spot she would fall madly in love with him. So he had to keep it covered with his hair.'

Andre held his hair from his forehead, leering, demanding, 'Kiss it, kiss it, kiss my love spot, my lovely ladies!'

They shrank back, laughing.

'What happened next, James?'

'One windy day the king's beautiful wife-to-be watched as the love spot was revealed by a gust that lifted Diarmuid's hair and she fell madly in love with him. They ran away together but they were followed by the king and his army as their love was forbidden. And so the couple became fugitives. They are still free and it is told that they roam around Ireland to this day.'

His companions clapped at the story and James bowed to them.

'And on that note of love and sadness I suggest we take a carriage to Montmartre to view our magnificent city from afar,' said Andre. 'Ladies?'

'You look very beautiful in your finery,' James said to Avril as they sat on the upholstered leather seat.

She did not respond to the levity in his tone, but held James' hand. 'Your hand is so soft,' she said quietly, and paused. 'Where have you been? I thought you might come back to see me again.'

He squeezed her hand, stroking it gently with the other as they talked. The carriage made its slow passage along the river and eventually the long climb to the Mount of Mars, where in olden days druids weaved their magic spells under Parisian skies of azure.

James and Avril lay close together on the grass as Andre walked arm in arm with his two companions, their voices trailing off as they moved further away. James stared at the sunny vista with a distant look in his eyes.

'Tell me what you are thinking,' whispered Avril, tickling his ear with a blade of grass.

'I am lost in dreams.'

'Oh,' she replied, 'what dreams are you lost in?'

He rolled over to face her, their bodies close, almost touching. 'I am walking in the sunshine through a wonderful valley. I feel happy. The birds are singing from the heart and the fragrance of this place is exquisite. Low hills on either side invite me upwards. I climb a hill, so soft, so yielding. And there, on the peak, I see a glade of flowers. In the centre is a rosebud, so delicious, so alluring. I approach, light as a butterfly. The petals sense me and open wide. I land. Where is it, where is the nectar I need so much to feed on, to suck until the flower is dry?'

Avril took James in her arms and he laid his head on her breast, breathing softly in the quiet stillness of the beautiful afternoon.

9

**To stop small creatures eating upon stored clothes
and linens**
Take a handful of small resin lumps of both frankincense
and myrrh. Place these within boxes or other storage
where any materials are kept. The precious substances are
easily availed of and will keep creatures away thanks to
their heady smell and perfume your linens nicely.

Quinn Household Recipes and Remedies Book

Paris, 2 January 1741

Dear Father and Mother,
*So now our course on man-midwifery has come to an end and I am
soon to leave Paris. How quickly the time goes, and how lucky
I have been to see the great city don the leaves on her trees like fine
dresses and then discard them as if disrobing for bed to sleep as the
seasons have passed.*

*I am so grateful for all your kindnesses of late, and those too
of Marguerite's mother and father. How can I ever repay Thomas
Lynch? Without him it would not have been possible to leave home
so that I could further my studies with such a sense of freedom from*

everyday constraints. I will be forever in his debt. As you said, he is a man with a sense of duty as strong as your own.

I have learned much during my time here. The Gregoires, the companion man-midwives, and the midwives themselves of the Hotel Dieu are so dedicated. I can hardly wait to begin my ambition to improve the fate of women and their unborn babies in our own fair country.

You will remember from my last letter that the Gregoires made an introduction for me to William Smyley, the man-midwife in London. He visited the Hotel Dieu a couple of years ago and continues to correspond with father and son. From what he writes, it appears that the midwifery services in London are not developed, a situation somewhat similar to Dublin.

And so now I am off to work with Smyley for six months in London. I hope to discover how I must run a service up to the standard of, or indeed better than his when I return to Dublin but without the good offices of the Gregoires and the Hotel Dieu to call upon. A daunting task lies ahead. Yet an exciting one, I'm sure you'll agree.

My good friend Andre gave me a special gift to remember my time in Paris. It is a first edition of The Byrthe of Mankynde *by Rosslin and translated from the German to English. The book is beautifully bound, a gilt edition that I shall treasure, and I do hope that Andre may come to visit so that I may bring him to Galway to meet you.*

From the start, my teachers advised me to diligently write out all my case studies and I accepted their advice. Father, just wait until you read the histories I have collected and written up in the journal you gave me, and with more to come in London. I could publish them as The Journals of a Man-Midwife.

Thank you for your letters with all the family news and events in Galway. Mother, your poor hand must be quite worn out by now, and I would say you are keeping food on the O'Malley table with the purchase of such large quantities of ink! Ah now, I can see your frown; you know well how I love to hear from you. I also hear from Thomas Lynch; he and Marguerite's mother miss her smiling, bright person most terribly – as do I.

One day I think I am finally starting to feel just a little content and then she visits me in a wisp of startling memory that I can't quite catch and hold in my hands. It can be a small thing: the dark hair of a girl as she passes by, the colour of a gown, it only takes a moment.

And my breath is snatched away and my heart is stolen all over again. I have come to welcome these occurrences as they make me feel close to her. I just wish I could reach out and take her to me, but it is not to be. I know she's there, I know she's near, I just can't hear her breathing.

Peg writes to tell me of our son, raising merry hell as he pulls things asunder here and there. A clever little one, then, to twist Peg and his carer Carissa O'Flaherty (whom I hear is doing admirably in her tasks, and doting on the boy – high praise indeed to come from Peg!) to his small whims.

I cannot wait to see him again, though I suppose he may be shy of his father. I will hold him and smell his sweet babyish self with joy in my very being. Peg also tells me, Mother, that Daniel loves the spinning top you sent to him, and claps delightedly with his small hands as he watches it turn, all the while asking for more. I am sure he would love another visit from you and Father, when you have the time, as I am to be absent for another while yet.

I must go now to send this letter, and one to my mentor Laurence Stone, who has been in regular contact and says that he awaits my return eagerly.

Love to you, Mother and you, Father, and to Kate. Tell her I will answer her letter at a later date – she is an author of such *lengthy missives that it will take me at least a week to set down all the replies needed!*

Your son,
James.

The frigid wind blew off the river and shook the bare trees that seemed to huddle around the great cathedral, just a few short steps away from the Hotel Dieu. The vast stones, statues and stained windows of Notre Dame were painted cream by the weak sun that shone through the wintry gloom on this feast day of the Epiphany, when the three wise men made their gifts to the baby that lay in a trough in a meagre stable, with only straw to soften his rest. A gargoyle sneered eternally, half at the heavens, half at humanity, which lay at its feet.

St Denis stood with his head under his arm, serene, flanked by angels and watching from his elevated height as people below scurried forward, cloaks clutched tightly against the wind, on their way to Mass.

Through the heavy wooden doors studded with huge, rust-coloured nails, on down the chill of the church's main aisle, on through to the sacristy, and with his hair highlighted by the sun that battled entry through the coloured window, motes dancing in the air, a boy unlocked a cupboard and lifted out a gold thurible.

He wore his fine serving robes this day: a red cassock under the bright white surplice with lace at the sleeves and at the knee, where the garment ended. His mother had chided him to keep it clean; she had spent hours washing and then starching it, she told him.

The thurible sat before the boy, its belly fat and its trinity of chains waiting to be lifted lying flat against it. The vessel was ready to be lit, so he got a taper and gently fed the flame to the charcoal waiting inside. He blew on it softly to make sure that it caught. He lifted the thurible by the chains and swung it back and forth to keep the slight ember glowing, and added the incense that gave the scent from the stable so many years ago, frankincense and myrrh.

The boy wondered if the aroma would evoke memories for Jesus, or if, being only a tiny baby at the time, it would make much of a difference at all. He watched as the wisping smoke rose to the heavens.

The priest watched the boy lost in his daydreams and started to ready himself for Mass. He donned the full-length white alb and tied it at his waist with a rope of the same colour to commemorate the bonds of Our Lord in captivity. He placed an amice around his neck and then the red silk chasuble, and he was ready to worship the Saviour.

The faithful crowded close to the altar, the choir began to sing the first hymn that tied the strands of the Mass together, and the priest stood, arms outspread, palms up. He joined his hands and started the ceremony.

Avril and James Quinn both sat quietly in a pew, breathing in the serene nature of their surroundings of the faithful at worship. The sun was coming through the painted glass, bathing the priest in heavenly light for the duration of his task.

As the music swelled around them, James looked to Avril, quiet beside him in contemplation or worship, he could not tell. He looked to the faithful singing their hearts out for God. He looked to one of the serving boys and thought of his own son at home. James hoped that

Marguerite would forgive him for treating the boy with such disinterest and blame at the start, in the cold, endless days after her death.

He needed her to forgive him, and as he sat he put his elbows on his knees and bent his head as a supplicant while he whispered his own prayers to her.

'Forgive me for Daniel. Forgive me for needing you so much that I was lost after you had gone and could not mind anyone let alone myself. Forgive me for a hundred other things, Marguerite, for I know you can see into my heart where they all lay.'

James Quinn looked up again and saw the crucifix where Jesus had given His life for the faithful, and thought of Marguerite who had given her life for her son. She had died on her own cross of agonies and he bent his head again with the thought and beseeched her for clemency.

Avril sat in her own reverie. Her bright hair was hidden from view and her body cloaked with a mantua. She turned her head and looked at James as he sat in prayer. She badly wanted to hold his hand, lying there warm and welcoming as his head was bent in concentration, she wanted to push the hair back from his forehead for him.

Kyrie eleison, Christie eleison, Kyrie eleison. Lord have mercy, Christ have mercy, Lord have mercy.

James thought the Greek verse discordant alongside the flowing Latin of the rest of the Mass, but joined Avril as she knelt for the incantation. The priest continued his dramatic performance for the Lord, treading the altar, dominating the large space in his capacity as God's representative on earth, holding the souls of the faithful in his hands as they bowed their heads behind him, ready to redeem or damn them for all eternity.

As the Mass continued, the choir singing, the priest's voice droning now, then grave and then joyful, Avril and James sat again and she regarded him. She knew she was a sinner. But then did Jesus not help Mary Magdalene, the Fallen Woman, just as James Quinn had helped her?

She hoped that she had given something back to him and a sigh escaped from her lips as the cries of 'Hosanna' echoed around their heads.

The boy entered the Mass from the back of the altar, holding the thurible reverently, flanked by the boat server, the holder of the silver incense container. The priest took the thurible from him and ladled more incense with a small spoon into its waiting mouth. He grasped the chains firmly and turned the instrument, clinking as he swung it towards the Blessed Sacrament three times, twice towards the crucifix and once to the altar, all the while intoning, praying, as the pungent aroma danced and skipped down the aisles and sat by the faithful.

'*Agnus Dei, qui tollis peccata mundi*; Lamb of God, who takes away the sins of the world. *Misere nobis*; Have mercy on us. *Dona nocis pacem*; Grant us peace.'

Avril bent her head and stifled a sob. The Mass was nearly ended, so too her time with James Quinn. He was leaving soon and she had asked to meet him here with her one last time. She wanted to tell him something, but was still unsure if she should, or hold her peace.

She prayed to the Blessed Virgin, 'Dear Lady, may your tears cleanse my soul. Forgive me. Help me to make my decision. Bless and mind James.' She felt a sliver of peace pierce her heart and knew that she would say nothing.

The Mass over, the boy cleaned out the remains of the charcoal and incense, sprinkling what was left over the earth from which roses would bloom in the garden at the back of the cathedral. He brushed the ashes from his hands, heeding his mother's words and keeping his robes clean, before heading back inside to his task of readying the thurible for the next ceremony.

Out of the boy's sight, a single ember smoked as James and Avril walked by. They stood outside the gates of the garden. She looked at the back of the glorious building, buttresses like petticoats peeking out from under a fine lady's voluminous skirts.

James took her face in his hands, gently, and looked into her eyes.

'If only,' she said, breath catching as a sob climbed its way up her throat, unbidden.

'I wish,' he started to reply and looked away.

'How can we?' she asked, and her voice sounded petulant to her own ears so she turned her head away from his hands.

He took her chin softly and turned her to face him again, finger raised and poised to touch the groove that ran from the bottom of her nose to the top of her lip as he had done before. 'Shush.'

She caught his finger mid-air, 'Please, James! Do not touch me there for I cannot bear it. I do not want to forget, I want to remember how it was.' She let his finger go and swayed for a moment, and he held out his hand to steady her.

'Are you feeling quite well, Avril? You look pale.' His concern was nearly her undoing.

'Just a little dizzy. I will be fine in a moment. I always am.' she knew then, as her shoulders straightened, that she would forge on alone. After all, she had been doing it for years. Newly resolved, she smiled up at him through the tears in her eyes.

'Go now, James. God be with you.' And she raised her hand in farewell and turned away before he could see the tears freely coursing down her cheeks. As she walked she laid her hand over her stomach and breathed deeply to try to dispel the weeping that threatened to overwhelm her.

The boy put the thurible back in the cupboard, locked it and patted the door of it behind him, satisfaction filling his belly at the thought that he had completed his task admirably.

The priest stood alone in the quiet of the echoing church, breathing in the atmosphere. He closed the missal and kissed it reverently where the gold cross shone bright on its cover. His eyes fell to the pew where Avril had sat. He looked on for a moment and then turned and walked away.

10

To still a vomit

The mithridate is often difficult to procure, given its long
list of ingredients, and some of these are hard to lay hold
of, such as opium, storax, agaric, spinkenard and costus.
Instead, to still and stay a sickening stomach, drink of a
pint of mint water, slowly. To make this, boil two handfuls
of mint leaves in fresh water, leave to cool and pour out.

Quinn Household Recipes and Remedies Book

LONDON, 1741

'So how do you like your calling now, James?' asked William
Smyley.

The night was pitch-black and James was exhausted and
cold beyond belief in the freezing January air. He only had
time to drop his bags and greet his host when word came
that they were needed. He followed Smyley on a borrowed
horse to a house where a woman had been labouring for
three days. She was exhausted and near the end.

William and James had done all they could in such a hopeless situation.

James leaned down and patted his mount on the neck. 'I was well warned by the Gregoires in Paris, that man-midwives are called too late in many cases, sir,' he replied.

'Now James, my name is William, not sir. Come and I will show you to your room and we will speak over breakfast.'

The next morning, the smell of baking bread woke James, and it took him a few moments to realise where he was. He dressed and washed hurriedly and made his way downstairs.

'Good morning, you must be James,' smiled a prettily plump woman as she took his hand. 'I am Eupham, William's wife. I am sorry I was not here to show you around myself last night but I was out with my charity work. At any rate, William says you were kept busy. Please, sit and eat,' she gestured to the table.

Once he was seated, her chatter continued. 'William is still asleep, so we can get to know each other a little before talk of medicine takes over.'

He smiled, taken with her and her friendly welcome.

'The Good Lord has not seen fit to grant us the grace of children, so William spends his time helping mothers and their babies. Have you a wife and children, James?'

'Sadly, most terribly, my own love died giving birth to our son, Daniel,' his face told the tale far better than any thousands of words.

Eupham put her hand over her heart and held the other out to James, a small pink thing on the snowy white tablecloth. 'I am so sorry. Was it long ago?'

James shook his head, recovered himself. 'Daniel is in his second year now. I don't see him as often as I should, but he is well minded at home. As for Marguerite, my heart, it will take me all my life to get over her passing.'

He cleared his throat. 'But tell me why you came to London from Scotland,' he smiled at Eupham once more.

'Now, James,' said William Smyley, finally roused from his bed, 'you may have things to do and people to see, but Eupham and I would like to bring you to the New Spring Gardens, Vauxhall, next Saturday for a special event to entice people to buy a yearly ticket. As such, I hear that all kind of things have been laid on to make people part with their money, so even though it is out of season we should have a good day there. It is not so far from us here at New Court, Pall Mall, being near the Lambeth Palace. Though if Eupham had her way she may take you off to the shops at the Royal Exchange, eh my dear?' he winked at James as his wife batted at him affectionately with her hand.

'The Gardens are such a lovely place,' said Eupham, her enthusiasm apparent. 'As you enter, you come across the most beautiful grove and then on to the Prince of Wales Pavilion, the central orchestra building, the supper boxes. Oh, and the most adorable life-sized statue of George Frideric Handel – he wrote the Vauxhall hornpipe don't you know – playing a lyre with tiny, perfect angels at his feet,' she clapped in glee as the men looked at her, pleased at her joy.

'The walks are gorgeous with arbours and flowerbeds full of every bloom in its season, it is a divine place for couples,' she smiled impishly at her husband. A dreamy look crossed her gentle features, her voice softened, 'and at dark the whole place is lit up with thousands of twinkling lights so it is like a magical fairytale night'.

She woke herself from her daydreams, looked to her husband and James, and clapped her hands together, once, briskly.

'Oh, I've kept you here while I've been nattering away. James, we would love your company. You will come, won't you?'

'I would like nothing more,' he replied, bowing his head to her.

She beamed at him, as pleased as a small child on receipt of an unexpected gift.

'And now, I am sure William wants to keep you busy!'

'Indeed, my dear, and our thanks for the glorious repast,' replied her husband, pecking her on the cheek as they passed.

James lifted his hand in a small gesture of goodbye, and she smiled at his retreating back as she bent to pick up the plates and cups. What a very nice young man. She tapped her bottom lip thoughtfully and paused in her task, smiling, then humming under her breath as she straightened and continued.

James Quinn felt ill as they disembarked from the barge that had transported them across the choppy waters of the Thames to the slimed and slippery stone steps at Vauxhall. He had never been the best of sailors, and the relentless swirling of the grey, greasy river had done him no favours.

'Are you feeling quite well, James?' asked Eupham, noting his pale face, sweat sheening his brow and beading his upper lip.

He looked down at her and shrugged off his queasiness with a smile. 'You would think, with all the journeys I have made, that a short crossing would be nothing to me, but I fear I have never gained my sea legs.'

'Oh well, the wind will soon clear your head and restore you,' she replied. 'Now, let us not tarry for I see William is keen to be at our destination.'

It was a short walk to the Vauxhall Gardens, and more people joined them as they neared there. The strains of music played by the Vauxhall Band coloured the air, and a sense of festivity rose about them.

As James and his companions passed, the band struck up the jaunty tune of 'The Dashing White Sergeant', and Eupham executed a tiny twirl in delight at her recognition of the Scottish song, light on her feet, skirts billowing around her dainty ankles.

Laughing, they went on, cheeks and noses reddened by the chill breeze, passing by the ticket sellers at the Pavilion.

'You go on, my dear, and I will purchase our entry,' said Smyley, stopping. 'James, would you escort my wife so no dashing youngster steals her away from me?'

James smiled at him. 'It would be my honour. Shall we?' He turned to Eupham, offering her his arm, and she nestled her small gloved hand cosily in the crook of his elbow.

They walked the length of the gardens, with her pointing out what plants and flowers would bloom later on, for the moment snug until spring under the dark soil blankets.

As Eupham and James ended the walkway and turned the corner, she cried out in alarm. There, in front of them, was a man lying on the cold earth as two brigands kicked him and shouted at him to reveal his possessions, which they were sure were about his person. The sickening sound of dull thuds reverberated as their booted feet connected with his prone body.

'Stop!' shouted James, and then he stepped back, taking Eupham with him as one of the men pointed a viciously sharp-looking knife at them, advancing, menace leaking through every pore.

But, at the sound of approaching footsteps and voices, the robbers left, leaving their quarry on the ground, his bright blood spilling out onto the bleak and barren earth.

Eupham stayed still where she was, weeping quietly as James ran to help the fallen man, casting glances at the poor wretch's wan face, his blood blossoming on the ground where no flower did.

'How are you faring, sir?' he asked gently as he helped the visibly shaken man to his feet. His nose was bloodied and he held his hands to his chest. 'Let me look at where you are hurt.'

The man nodded in numb assent; Eupham watching on as James ran his hands gently over the injured man.

'My name is James, James Quinn.'

'And I am Alan Cavendish.'

The man tried to straighten up, but the pain was too great.

'Take your ease, we can get acquainted later,' replied James, laying his hand on the man's back.

After James gave a description of the vagabonds to the constable who was on duty at the Gardens and who had arrived at the scene quickly, he turned to Eupham and Smyley, who stood in quiet stillness.

'I must help this poor man home. I am sorry to leave; maybe we could all come again in spring and see the blooms in their finery as you described to me earlier.'

'Of course, James, you must go. I am quite recovered and William will take me for tea, won't you William, hot and strong and full of sugar. Bless you, James. We will see you later and my thanks to you for minding me so well.'

'Any time, my dear lady,' he answered, taking her hand and kissing it gently.

'Thank you indeed,' said a shaken William Smyley, grasping James's hand and holding it in gratitude before letting go and gathering his wife to him.

As James entered through the gates of the injured man's home, his breath was taken away by the grand, imposing house, which stood not far from Lambeth Palace.

'You are a kind young fellow,' said Alan Cavendish, patting James's hand, 'I am most indebted to you.'

'I will not be happy 'til I see you resting in bed,' he replied.

So the two men made their slow way up the steps to the impressive abode, the older man breathing heavily and leaning on James for support.

When inside, the uniformed butler, once over his shock at his master's condition, helped the two men up to the bedchamber, and they laid the injured man down gently on the fine covers of his bed. The butler bowed, and with a 'please ring the bell if you need me Sir Alan,' left the room, looking over his shoulder at the young man crouched before his master.

Sir Alan groaned as James touched his sore flesh here and there, noting the dried blood at his nostrils and the red mark around his right eye that would surely purple and blacken by the morning. His ribcage was tender and knees scraped.

'Sir Alan,' James tested the words ruefully, 'I am glad you told me of your status so I could be on my best behaviour!

'I believe some ribs have been broken during your attack. This would explain your great difficulty in breathing. I wish to visit an apothecary to purchase some pain-relieving laudanum which will relax you.'

James smiled at his patient and patted his hand. 'And in the meantime, do me the great honour of staying in your bed until I get back. Sir.'

'As if I could even rise, young man,' replied Sir Alan, sharp, painful coughs rising as he held his ribs to him.

Once the laudanum was administered, his patient fell into a grateful slumber, breathing easier as the drug coursed through his body, the sharp look of pain lessening and then leaving his features.

'Give him more if he needs it later,' James said to the butler who hovered solicitously around the doorway of the bedchamber. 'I shall write down instructions for dosage and where you can contact me if Sir Alan has any worries or excessive pain. I will return in the morning to see how he is.'

Having done so, he left the fine home and went out into the dreary, darkening London evening, tightening his coat around him as he walked, the gathering gloom swallowing him from sight.

James fidgeted as he waited outside the highly glossed door with the lion's head knocker, feline mouth open, showing wickedly sharp teeth and plump tongue, mane in disarray as it roared in perpetual silence. He pulled at his collar, which felt too tight, but Eupham had insisted on checking him before he left the Smyley house this evening, brushing the shoulders of his coat with nimble fingers.

'Now don't you look just fine,' she said, smoothing his unruly hair from his forehead, stepping back and clucking her tongue like a mother hen. 'Just fine.'

The grandly embossed copperplate invitation had arrived a few days previously, heavy cream card luscious in his hand, requesting his attendance at a family gathering thrown in his honour for helping Sir Alan Cavendish that day at the Vauxhall Gardens.

James combed his hair with his fingers as the door opened to admit him.

He stood in the hall, taking in the details: the mirrors, ancestral portraits, the grand, sweeping staircase, the multitude of candles in gold sconces adorning the walls.

'This way, sir, if you please,' the butler smiled at him and lead him to the drawing room where the guests were assembled in their finery, the fire burning merrily at the grate, casting brilliant light over the space as it leaped off the crystal candelabras.

Sir Alan rose and crossed the room to James, taking both hands in his and clasping them warmly, firmly.

'And so, here is my rescuer!' he turned to the assembled crowd, 'Doctor James Quinn, my friends. Now before I introduce you, will you have some wine?'

'No sir, thank you, some tea perhaps?'

'Indeed, young man, it is better to keep a clear head in your case, as you never know who will be in need of your urgent assistance at any given time!' laughed Sir Alan, his guests taking their cue as amusement spread through the room.

'You look improved, Sir Alan; I hope you feel it too.'

'Ah yes, much better, because of your quick actions. Now, come and meet my dear friends and family.'

James followed his host around the sumptuous room, shaking hands, complimenting, passing on to the next person, until before him stood one of the most exquisite beings he had ever seen. Dark hair piled high on her head, jewels nestled and shining within. Blue stones on her ears and at her throat, a profusion of darker blue velvet, brocade and lace covering her shapely body. Her ruby lips curved in smile, eyes bright and mischievous.

'And so, James, the jewel in my crown, I present to you my daughter Catherine, one of London's most glittering and sought-after residents. Artists, actors and musicians, among others, leave their cards on a daily basis, and she is the toast of the Kit-Cat Club.'

'How charming to meet you,' she said, 'and that was quite the introduction, Father.' She held her hand to James to be kissed. He took it, noting the large blue ring on her finger, testing the warmness of her and raising her hand to his lips, and bending down he mouthed, 'The pleasure is all mine.'

'Catherine, look after my rescuer, dear, while I see to our other guests.'

She smiled and nodded to her father.

'So, Doctor Quinn. James. May I call you that? My father and I are indeed indebted to you. I am glad it was not me there, for I do not know what I would have done. I do not have a protector, as such, as my dear husband, an army officer, was killed in a horse-riding accident near on six years ago, so it is very reassuring to know that there are kind gentlemen such as yourself out there who may protect a lady – and her father,' she said, and tapped her Chinese fan against her open palm. 'We never did have children,' she paused and looked at him intently. 'Father tells me you have a little son? Do you spend much time with him?'

He shook his head, 'Sadly not, for I have been abroad much recently. But Daniel is well minded at home.'

'Ah but you should see him,' said Catherine, 'especially since he has no mother. A child needs at least one parent, I should know that,' she looked at her father across the room and bestowed a dazzling smile on him. 'Our own mother died when my sister Alice was born – a great loss of blood, I think? And even though we have other women in our lives, aunts and the like, it was always Father we turned to with our childish scrapes and woes. So you see, James, once you make a bond with Daniel it will never be broken.'

II

To make an orange pudding
Add to the yolks of ten eggs a quart of rich cream and
half a pound of orange peels. Mix these well and sweeten
to your taste. Melt half a pound of butter and put into
your mixture. When smooth and not too runny pour out
into a serving dish.

Quinn Household Recipes and Remedies Book

James was not seated beside Catherine at dinner, but
glanced at her often in between mouthfuls of Cheshire
cheese, pigeon pie, syllabub and finally a soft orange
pudding. She caught his eye through the candles that sat
in their fine holders on the highly polished table top and
smiled at him; their reflections smiled back at them. He, a
little embarrassed to be caught, turned with haste to her
plump laughing sister Alice on his left, or her somewhat
dour, pinched-face aunt on his right.

He heard Catherine's vivacious chatter throughout the
meal and was glad when they were asked to rise from their
carved chairs and go back to the drawing room for musical
entertainment.

Catherine sat on the stool in front of the fine new

pianoforte. He had heard of the instrument but had never seen one before, and she seemed to his eyes to become one with the instrument, the candlelight catching the jewels in her hair, making them blink as she bent before the ivory notes, fine fingers raised then lowered. And as the beautiful notes wafted around the room, light and translucent as butterfly wings on the air, James felt himself transported, and looking round saw that the other guests did too.

As she paused to take a break, the sound of the flickering fire took over, warm and sleepy.

'Catherine, play "The Sweet Maid of Notting Hill"!' beseeched Alice.

Sibling smiled at sibling and Catherine once again bent her head and put her fingers to the keys. As the opening bars continued, she sang and the sweetest notes filled the air.

She sang of a simple shepherd and his love for a sweet, wealthy girl, her voice trilling, expressing the feelings of the tale, joyful with hope and then sad as the shepherd realises that he and his darling may never be together.

James sat enraptured, taken over by her voice, warmth swelling within him, amazed at her talent for bringing the story to life.

Silence again, and then the assembled guests clapped their hands vigorously. She declined to play any more, pleading a break before her poor fingers quite fell off. Laughter echoed around the grand room once more.

'She would be a wonderful catch for you, dear boy,' said Sir Alan to James as they stood together.

'Father!' Catherine turned to Sir Alan, 'Not that again!' She looked at James. 'Father is always trying to marry me off to some boring aristocrat,' she eyed him speculatively and tapped him on the arm with her fan. 'But you are neither, I think, so you must have made a really good impression for him to want me to spend the rest of my life with you,' she jested.

'This time, my dear, I joke not,' said Sir Alan. 'Your mourning time is long past and I long for some grandchildren to play with in my older age. But now James, come and tell my guests and I of your upcoming plans for your time in London.'

James looked over his shoulder at her as he was led away.

'So James had you not seen a pianoforte before?' asked Catherine as they sat in the Cavendish drawing room that fine February morning which had an early hint of spring. The fire jumped cheerfully in the grate.

'I confess that I had not, and more's the pity. I must say, you play wonderfully well.'

'Surely you have seen a clavichord or a harpsichord?'

'Not only that but with one hand I can play "An Cailín Deas, The Lovely Lady", slowly of course, with much hesitation and deliberation,' he smiled at her and she laughed, making a shooing motion with her be-ringed hand.

'Well, the piano, as you know, is the newest instrument of our time – and it is based on both the organ and the clavichord.'

'And do you play the organ?'

'Only on special occasions, but it is truly stirring in the right setting, is it not?' she asked him, corners of her mouth curled upwards, showing off her small white teeth. 'You do know the organ is of ancient design?'

'I did not, I confess, tell me more,' he replied softly and looked deeply into her blue eyes, noticing the darker flecks there.

'Stop it, I tell you, stop,' she laughed at him. 'Don't flirt with me because my father will sell me off to the highest bidder!'

Their laughter subsided.

'Tell me about the design of the organ,' he said.

Catherine stood and picked up an English flute from the instruments beside the piano, handled it lightly and put it to her lips, pausing, then looked at James.

'The Greeks had pipes, a little like this flute. They placed seven of them with different tones side by side and blew them with a pump, and so they created the hydraulis, the Greek organ. The piano you see here is based on the best features of the organ, clavichord and harpsichord.' She stopped, twirled the flute in her hand and looked at him from under her lashes. So do I make a good teacher?'

He nodded, motioning, 'And these are the keys?'

'Of course, dear pupil, they attach to little hammers covered with soft felt that knock on the strings. The string vibrates and makes its own sweet sound,' she pressed down lightly and hummed the same note as the depressed key before lifting her finger off it.

'And for loud or soft, how does that work?'

'The keys respond to my touch, so, light.'

'Or firm?'

'As you say – here let me play for you.'

Catherine sat before the gleaming, waxed instrument and placed her fingers on the keys.

She took a moment as if pondering what to play for him, cleared her throat and bent her head, exposing her white neck and her dark clinging curls to him in doing so.

Her fingers flew over the keys, swooping, sliding, and resonating over the wings and soundboard.

As Catherine finished the piece and the last lingering notes softened into silence she looked over at James, who was sitting thoughtfully, quietly.

'That was an inspired performance from my magnificent teacher,' he said. '*Bravissimo*, Catherine.'

Flushed, she smiled at him and patted the piano stool, 'Join me, James, we will do it together. Let us play a duet.'

He sat and she looked at him seriously.

'Here, put your fingers as I show you. You will play the easy part. I will help you.'

She placed his fingers correctly on the keys. 'Show me your hand, here, but lightly. First comes the chord of F major; then slowly stretching to reach the G position, follow by a lift to A minor; return but easily to F and finally the perfect chord. Play it, James, here for me from this key, from the middle C.'

Catherine opened her eyes to the sight of her candlelit bedchamber, and pulled the covers snug up under her chin. She sighed in the night's stillness. She blew out the candle and lay her head on the plump pillow.

'*Bravissimo*, Catherine,' she whispered to the darkness.

'Here are the case notes for our house visits,' Smyley passed the pages to James as they sat in the study. 'They are all within easy distance from us here by horse – Gerrard Street, Wardour Street, the East End and on to the docks.'

He picked a piece of lint from the arm of his chair, rolled it between his fingers and flicked it to the ground. 'Forgive my loose hand; I always appear to be in a hurry and my writing tells it so,' he smiled at James.

'Not copperplate, my word, and me here to learn from

the master! I pray that I may endeavour to interpret them,' James parried, and bent his head to read, a smile on his face, as Smyley's handwriting was as bad as promised.

He looked up some time later to see William Smyley coming towards him, sturdy leather pannier in one hand.

'In here, James,' he patted the makeshift case affectionately, 'I place my blunt hook, a fillet, a lever and crochet, accompanied by scissors, lancets and my obstetric forceps. When out visiting patients I must carry all my requirements with me. Follow me down the house now and we shall pick up some treatments.'

On the ground floor William opened the door to a side room he used as an apothecary shop for his drug dispensing. Rows of neatly labelled bottles and containers stood on the shelves.

'The contents are as expected, James. I refill the containers each evening,' and he smiled as he picked up another pannier, this one full of remedies.

In the hallway, Eupham handed William his cloak and kissed him on the cheek. 'Stay warm, my dear. And you too, James.'

'Expect us late home,' Smyley replied, gave her hand a squeeze and went out the door to where the horses stood, James following.

The men chatted amiably as they rode. The horses snorting, the cold air pluming their breaths into great wreathing clouds, panniers laid over their rumps.

On through the city they rode, past Lincoln's Inn Fields, the Strand, Drury Lane and into Clare Market. The smell of meats assailed James's nose, the ground slippery under the horses' hooves, splattered as it was with innards and slick with blood and mucous here and there. An old crone stared up at him sightlessly; one rotten tooth stood lonely in her mouth as she held up an indefinable piece of raw meat to James, like a glorious offering in her gnarled paw. He hastened to catch up with Smyley, his horse losing its footing as he urged it forward over the slippery, frozen red ground.

They turned into Vere Street and stopped. William dismounted and rapped sharply at a door. Midwife Lee opened it and peered out to see who it was, relief crossing her face as she saw them.

'Dr William, she is in great need. Her piles are most woeful!' she said and ushered the men in.

Mrs Lacey stood by the dirty window wringing her hands in distress, belly straining her garments, pulling them taut.

'She is eight months gone with her second child, and constipated when she goes to the stool. She has dreadful discomfort in her nether regions and dung gate for two days past,' the midwife explained. 'Excuse me for saying, but the piles are so gross in size they appear like cauliflowers for all the world, rotten cauliflowers all red and black.'

'If gross excrement retained in the right gut be the cause of it,' William opined, 'an emollient enema of the decoction of mallows, pellitory, violets and oil of sweet almonds with fresh butter could be helpful.'

Midwife Lee looked doubtful.

'Or you may anoint the piles with an anodyne remedy,' offered James, 'with hot stroking from the cow or linseed oil well beaten with water lilies, poppies and white broth mixed with the yolk of an egg and ground in a leaden mortar.'

'Either way, we should examine and then prescribe,' William reflected.

The midwife walked the suffering woman from the window, laid her on the pallet bed, and lifted her skirts and petticoats high as she faced her to the wall.

The woman cried out in pain, though the examination that followed was gentle. William and James exchanged glances with Midwife Lee. Simple diet and medications would not be sufficient to relieve the problem.

'A draught of pain-relieving elixir and then the lancet, methinks,' remarked William. 'We must incise the haemorrhoids and release the retained blood clots.'

The woman shrank away from them in alarm, whimpering, her piles being so sore as to forbid any touch, however tender.

'Then we should apply a decoction of rinds of pomegranate and province roses made with smith's water and alum, to which is added dragon's blood and terra sigillata,' mused James before he moved off to one side with William as the woman drank the elixir that had been handed to her.

'There is another option,' he said quietly, out of earshot.

'I agree,' William replied with conviction.

As the mixture of brandy and opium – the laudanum of Paracelsus – took hold, the suffering woman relaxed and her shoulders slumped as though a great weight had been lifted from them.

William removed a jar from his pannier and looked at the Hirudo medicinalis creatures within as they sat in their slimy residue, a limpid, dark, softly seething mass. He lifted one out, holding it away from himself with finger and thumb, and looked at it as it wriggled slowly in his grasp.

With great care, the man-midwives gently applied twenty of the blood-sucking leeches to the hard fleshy areas of the prone woman's piles and close by on her nether regions.

The creatures would do their job well, as organised as a small shadowy army, clinging on, feeding. As they gorged on the woman's retained blood, they would bloat to many times their original size and then fall to the bed, replete with their magnificent meal, large black stains on the pale sheets.

The piles would bleed for a time yet, and more Hirudo would replace them, their sated brothers and sisters at rest again in the glass jar.

'Tomorrow, on our return, there will be a change for the better. I will fit a small end of a pullet's gut on a pipe and place the instrument deep in the fundament to apply a clearing enema. After that we must arrange a suitable diet,' said William Smyley to Midwife Lee. She showed them to the door and out into the frigid day before turning back to her patient.

It was late afternoon by the time William and James reached the tenement where Mrs Roberts lay, tears standing shining in her great, sunken eyes.

'Her fever has lessened,' said Midwife Peake, 'but the pain in her breast grows ever more.'

Their journey had taken them into the mean, mired streets of the city, and it was with cloaks gathered tightly to them and horses needing to be calmed constantly against the woeful pleas of the disaffected that they turned off the wide street of Bishopsgate, past the London Workhouse in Half Moon Alley and on to their destination.

Mr Roberts was at his employment, while his children sat disconsolately in the tiny, barren room that served as kitchen and living quarters, shivering in the bitter cold, not talking or playing as ones their age should.

The tiniest child whimpered, her hair hanging lank in front of her eyes, breath whispering cloudy in the air, dirty feet and hands kissed blue by the cold. She drew her feet up under her skirts to try and warm them, toddler arms hugging herself, their plumpness taken too early by meagre rations. She sniffled and coughed as her siblings sat mute.

Mrs Roberts was huddled on a low bed in the chamber that was shared by the whole family, plus one, now that the new baby was here.

James and William walked towards her, the sickly sweating pale shadow of a woman and the crying baby that lay close by, tiny fists in the air, railing against the injustice of it all.

The men examined her gently. William pressed lightly with his fingertips on her inflamed breast, branded with a large red swelling on the pale flesh crossed with blue raised veins, and the woman winced and cried out in pain.

'See there, the abscess has ripened,' said James.

'Just there,' replied William, pointing with his index finger, 'the centre is a little elevated and very soft so that it fluctuates. My experience in matters surgical is somewhat less than yours, James, but I feel the time is right to proceed.'

The two moved to a corner of the glum room.

'We must use the lancet to make an incision in the form of a half moon. The cut must be large enough to ensure that we can evacuate all the purulent material while taking care not to open any great blood vessels.'

'The vessels are mainly to the side are they not?'

James nodded. 'Once drained, the abscess cavity should be cleansed. Tents or pledgits of lint dipped in oil of eggs or basilicon mixed with a digestive should be placed in the hollow that remains to fully purge the area.'

'What of the other breast?' enquired William.

'I did not detect the presence of an abscess. However, the nipple is chafed and excoriated. We should apply honey of roses and put a little cap of wax or wood over the area so that the woman's clothes may not stick to it. When the crisis is at end she may draw the nipple out with a fit instrument of glass or have another woman suck the teat to draw it out to fullness so that she may be able to feed again.'

12

To keep a good flow of milk in nurses and to ensure its goodness
Make a broth with lentils to which add ale, aniseed, barley, cinnamon, beaten eggs, parsnip, sugar, rice and wheat. A handful of each and a cup of ale will suffice. Mix with enough water to cover it, boil it to soften and pour off to cool. Let her drink freely of it.

Quinn Household Recipes and Remedies Book

James laid out the lancet, lint pledgits and jars of medicines while Mrs Roberts swallowed great spoonfuls of pain-relieving elixir, taking a thin finger and wiping up any liquid that spilled down the side of her mouth before placing the digit in her mouth and sucking to the last drop.

When content that the medicine was working, William and the midwife held the woman tightly. She squirmed under their hands, head twisting from side to side as her dirty hair snaked its way over the pillow.

James grasped her right breast firmly in his left hand, made the incision, and then plunged the lancet deep, releasing a putrid stream of pus, which made its way yellowly down her side. Mrs Roberts collapsed into a deep faint while James completed the task of cleansing, insertion of medicated compresses and binding of the breast.

Together with the midwife, James and William cleaned the mess and stayed with Mrs Roberts until she was so improved that she could sit up and ask for a drink, gabbering away in her relief, calling to the toddler in the other room to come for a cuddle, crooning in the child's ear once she did, holding her as the child smiled and looked up at the strangers.

'Now, as to feeding of your baby,' started Smyley.

'Well now, Doctor, I have that all seen to,' said Midwife Peake and called out. A woman who had been waiting outside came into the room, the wet nurse. Rose by name, slim but well nurtured, dressed shabbily, but most importantly, clean. They questioned her, as she shifted and circled a booted foot on the floor.

James placed her age at about thirty as she herself was quite uncertain. Her own baby was almost four months old so there was no doubt but her milk was purified by now. Her womb had ceased its loss of discharge from the birth for some weeks past. Further questions revealed that her courses had not returned, neither was she with child as she had not yet lain with her husband.

In response to their further queries, it transpired that Rose was not subject to the king's evil, nor any hereditary disease. She had no spot, nor the least suspicion of any venereal distemper, nor itch, scab, scald or other filth of like nature.

The midwife had chosen Rose for her dark hair, which meant that her milk would not be hot, sharp or evil smelling. Her teeth were in good enough order, William nodded happily as they looked in her mouth as she would no doubt often kiss the child while feeding and infect his tiny lungs if her breath was corrupted. No scars were present on her breasts, another good omen, and she had not been struck down with a breast abscess in the past. Rose was broad and her breasts were of good size, firm and strong as it was some hours since she had last fed her own child. The nipples were well shaped, of good texture and firm to the touch.

'We must test the milk now,' said James.

So Rose milked onto the midwife's hand, pulling softly at her breast and nipple in imitation of a suckling infant. They judged the appearance of the milk not too watery nor too thick, and of good colour and fragrance. The midwife turned her hand slowly and the milk slid off gently.

She nodded to Rose and the woman milked again into a small pewter spoon, which was passed around and tested.

'The milk is sweet and sugared without any acrimony or other strange taste,' said James as William smiled at Midwife Peake.

'You have chosen well,' he said to her, 'but what of–'

'Her temperament is without fault: not quarrelsome nor melancholy but merry and cheerful, not given to gin nor excess of the pleasures of Venus.' The midwife, well versed, knew what he had been about to ask.

'Altogether the qualities we seek in a good wet nurse,' William smiled at her once more. 'Midwife Peake, we shall return again in three days' time to check on your small charge and his mother.'

As the men left, James looked back to see the baby cradled in Rose's arms, cheeks working furiously as it sucked deeply from her, satisfying his tiny body with the wholesome liquid, cries ceased.

James and William returned to the house in high spirits, James to write a letter home and William to write notes for the classes that he offered to both male and female midwives.

'Eupham, are you home?' shouted out William. 'Eupham?'

She came out into the hall, eyes red from weeping, a piece of paper in her hand that she quickly hid behind her back.

'Eupham, my dear, what is it? Are you not well?' said Smyley, moving towards her.

She took a step back. 'It is nothing William,' her voice faltered.

'What are you holding behind your back?' he asked.

'Oh. Oh, it is nothing, nothing at all!' she replied.

'Well then, let me see it.'

'No, William.'

'Eupham!'

James took in the scene uncomfortably. He knew enough of his hosts by now to see that this argument was out of character for them both and it made him feel incredibly tense. He was about to make his escape when William turned Eupham and pulled the piece of paper out of her hand.

As his eyes scanned it he turned red, and then pale, and then the colour suffused his face again and the paper in his hand trembled. He let it fall to the floor. It fluttered gracefully like a leaf from a tree in October, before reaching the wood below. He strode out of the hall and they heard a door slam behind him.

James approached Eupham. She was trembling and crying again.

'Come Eupham, let us sit and I will make us some tea and we can talk if you wish.'

She picked the piece of paper from the floor and balled it tightly in her fist.

Once they were seated, James opened her fist, took the damp paper from her hand and smoothed it out, laying it on the table. He read and his heart sank. It was a pamphlet, crudely written and crudely drawn to be sure, but its intent was unmistakable.

He looked up at Eupham who had her face buried in a large white handkerchief, from behind which her distress was audible. His teacher, William Smyley, was depicted wearing a nightgown of flowered calico with a nightcap of office, tied with pink and silver ribbon. Under it was written, 'Would you have this man at your bed as you deliver forth a child?'

'Oh Eupham,' said James, 'I think you had better tell me.'

She took the handkerchief from her face and James walked around to her side of the table and sat beside her, taking her hand. She turned her blotched face to him. 'I am so angry, and sad, and one hundred other things I cannot put into words,' she said tremulously at first, her voice growing as she went on. 'William is such a good man! He cares for the poor, cares too much sometimes. He pays for much of it himself, did you know that? We pay for it. It is just as well we have no extra mouths to feed in our own home or our children would surely starve to death!' she gulped. 'Oh, I have said too much,' and she burst into another noisy bout of crying.

'Eupham,' said James, his arm around her shoulder, 'this is just spite. Hurtful as it is, spite. You and William are among some of the kindest, best people I know, and it would honour me to call you my friends.'

She turned her face to him and smiled through her tears. 'You are a caring man, James, and a good friend, but there has been worse, you know, much worse,' and she told him her woes.

James knocked at William's study door and entered. William was sitting in a chair, the sleek black house cat on his lap. The cat lifted his head at James's approach. James looked at Smyley's miserable face. Down the small panes of glass behind his head the daylight lowered. And as James sat down opposite him, his host's hair was illuminated from behind a small occasional table, giving him the appearance of prophetic greatness, haloed as he was.

Smyley stroked the cat, which responded to his hand with rippling fur and pleasured purrs. 'The cat is called Abraham,' he said. 'Eupham ladles her love on him, calls him Baby Bram – I don't think the grizzled old gentleman from the Bible would have approved, do you? At any rate, she needs an outlet for all her love and affection. I myself am drowned in it on a regular basis.' He paused and looked at James.

'She was trying to protect me, James.'

James nodded his understanding and let the words spill from Smyley.

'Unlike some of my colleagues, I do not speak ill of the midwives who live in this part of London. I meet with them and keep good work relations with many of them. Most of my efforts come from their good offices. Now you can understand why I will welcome women and midwives to my courses readily, so all may study equally.'

'Yet Eupham told me that you are pilloried in the press by midwives who find the presence of the man-midwife unnecessary at delivery. She was very upset,' James said, recalling her unhappy face, normally wreathed in smiles and good nature.

'I am written about in many pamphlets, did she tell you that?' Smyley stiffened and the cat jumped from his lap, looking back at him disdainfully, tail kinked in a question mark at his usually mild-mannered master's change of mood. It meowed as if in rebuke and stalked away to the fireside to lay down once more.

William paused and the bright flush of annoyance sank from his cheeks. 'I made a well-intentioned proposal to soften the prejudice against the man-midwife. We could wear a commodious dress like a loose nightgown over our clothing when proceeding to a delivery. You see where my comments have led today.'

He gave a great sigh and looked to the fire. 'A notable midwife wrote that I am a great horse of a man with hands so large no gloves can be made to fit.' Smyley, wounded, took a handkerchief from his pocket, shook it out crisply and blew his nose noisily into it before squeezing it in his hand.

'Worse still, of a number of colleagues wrote cruelly about me. One said that my hands are only fit to hold horses by the snout while they are shod by the farrier, or they may be used to stretch boots in Cranburn Lane! I try to shield Eupham from such insulting remarks, as she becomes inflamed on my behalf. She would like me to write a pamphlet in my own defence but I am not sure that is the best way.'

The room fell full and heavy with silent thought, both men gazing at the flames as the cat opened a sleepy yellow eye and regarded them.

Dublin, 26 February 1741

Dear Doctor James,
I am very glad to hear that your time in London is proving a success and that you will be coming back to us later this year. Thanks for your letter.

Thanks too for the book for Daniel, though I think if you don't mind me saying so but Mr Defoe's The Life and Strange Surprising Adventures of Robinson Crusoe, of York, Marnier *is a little beyond his comprehension and age at the moment.*

Perhaps if you were to find a book about animals before you return? They are Daniel's favourite things at the moment and on walks woe betide if we do not stop to say hello to every cat, dog or horse we may encounter.

We read the book you have sent every night at bedtime before the candle is blown out. And your son, being a such bright inquisitive little dote with the word 'why' coming up in our talks many times a day every day, wants to know about the sea and boats and why did Mister Crusoe do this or that. I must confess I do not always have the answers!

But it is very difficult to get exasperated at his curious little face turned upwards towards my own as he waits as patiently as he can for the reply to his questions.

We go to the park on fine days, and he is fascinated by the other children there, especially as he regards himself as such a big boy whenever we see a child younger than him, or a baby.

He has a smile that lights up a room and a laugh that would gladden the stoniest heart. Much like his mama.

He is nearly able to put on his own shoes now, and we have a rhyming song for the task which he hums under his breath throughout the day.

And as for his drawings! Why, I am very impressed by his hand – for one that is so young he shows a fine grasp of things and people and colours. I am sending you a recent picture. Daniel did it for you, but I feel I must tell you, and do not mean any hurt by it, that he does not remember you, as you are only ever presented as a shadowy figure, present in his life yet not. I lay no blame, indeed I would never presume to do so, but tell you that you should be aware so that on your return you can start anew with your son.

We are all well here in Dublin, and look forward to your return. Please let me know if there is anything that you would like me to do before you arrive, and wishing you a safe and speedy journey.

Yours,
Peg Reilly.

James Quinn ran his finger over the crudely drawn cat, coloured a bright, improbable blue, and smiled. The feline had startling red eyes and enormous, jagged teeth. If Peg thought this was a great talent who was he to argue?

And suddenly he felt so homesick that he could taste it. He sighed and wished with all his heart that he was back in Dublin with his small son, finally making a relationship with him.

London, 11 March 1741

Dear Father and Mother,
I hope this finds you well, and thanks to you and Kate for the last letters from home. You must tell her it took me at least a week to read her writings!

I have had a letter from Peg with a picture from Daniel. My, what an artist at such a tender age! I find myself yearning for him and look forward greatly to getting home to see my boy.

London still enthrals me. I have enjoyed my time here and have learned and seen much.

The Gregoires warned me well – those differences that exist in medical care between London and Paris are truly astonishing. Paris has been at the forefront for centuries and as yet London does not follow its lead. There is no charity ward in all of London for women in childbirth, can you believe that? No charity ward; my anger rises up through my body in waves of coursing heat at the thought, may the Lord bless the women and children of this city. Of course Dublin and even our own dear Galway are no better, but having seen the light of wisdom in Paris it is difficult to return to the dark again.

Here in London, the Royal Hospitals of St Bartholomew and St Thomas and also Guy's Hospital minister to the sick and dying. There is the new London Infirmary for the manufacturing classes and merchant seamen, Greenwich Hospital for sailors, and even Bedlam for the insane. Do mothers and their infants not count at all?

Still, there is one man-midwife, Richard Manningham by name, who tries to emulate the Paris tradition. He has set up a small charitable ward for mothers in houses along Jermyn Street.

William fears the noble venture will soon be submerged under waves of debt for want of public funds. Meanwhile, the city is overtaken and swimming in gin.

William Smyley is such a great man. His practice here is as mine will be in Dublin. There are rounds of the patients in the districts each morning and afternoon.

The evening is taken up with writing the day's cases and preparing for the visitations on the following day. In the midst of this medley come the urgent calls both day and night to attend difficult and unresolved midwifery cases. Such is the life of the modern man-midwife. William and the Gregoires seem happy with the lives they have chosen. I hope that after all my studying and hard work I will be as satisfied with mine.

I must remain here until June, at the latest, to complete my preparations for my new life as a man-midwife in Dublin. By then I will be very excited to see Daniel and come to visit you in Galway. I must confess I cannot wait!

With love, I enclose my affection for you all at home within the folds of this letter.

Your son,
James.

13

To make your own ass's milk when there is no beast at hand

Take a fine handful of the roots of the sea holly and add to it some pearl barley. Boil these in fresh water until much reduced. Strain the mixture off to cool and then add some fresh boiled cow's milk and stir. Drink anytime when most agreeable, but particularly in the morning.

Quinn Household Recipes and Remedies Book

The early afternoon sunlight filtered in through the windows, lighting even the darkest corners of the wood-panelled games room. It gifted the sporting paintings with bright achievement and snuggled into the seats of the soft chairs along the walls as if resting there for a moment. The rectangular wooden-framed billiard table stood proudly in the middle of the room, with cue holder, ball holder and the famous rules book *The Complete Gamester* by Charles Cotton within easy reach of whoever decided to play. Card tables sat in a small alcove off Sir Alan Cavendish's favourite room.

'The billiard game is not your forte, James,' Sir Alan smiled as he replaced the cues then spun the ivory ball down the green cloth.

'Time was always against me,' he replied wryly. 'My studies first, then work filled my life. There has been precious little time for entertainment.'

'So unlike Mary Queen of Scots, who was laid out in repose on the billiard table cloth she loved so well, it appears you have no such intent.' Sir Alan paused. 'You live a strange life, my friend, devoted to the lives of others, and the welfare of mothers and infants. Me, I do not venture to understand women and their foibles although I do find their race infernally delightful.

'All that work around the house and dressing and stitching and crochet must be dreadfully boring. Give me the hounds and the hunt, the sport and carousing and the better things in life like a good card game with friends.'

Sir Alan looked around the room, glancing at each painting in turn, as if weighing his words on his tongue before speaking again.

'Meanwhile you delve under the skirts and petticoats of women seeking Lord knows what, maybe even the future in the crystal ball that is the matrix.'

'The Good Lord placed the womb in that location under the skirts, Sir. Otherwise it might be attached to the chest, a knee or an elbow.' James's reply painted seams of mirth on his host's face. 'The Ancients were of the opinion that the womb was forever on the move. One day here, close to the fundament, another day wandering up here under the breast bone.'

Sir Alan countered, 'So you, like Doubting Thomas with his finger in the wound of Jesus, must constantly seek proof of their error.' He laughed at his own response. 'I tease you, James, it is but a jest. Here let us sit awhile before we join Catherine and her visitors. It will make for an interesting evening as the guests are from the worlds of art, music and the theatre – trust Catherine to provide us with stimulating conversation over the dinner table!'

As the men sank into the plush seats, Sir Alan's conversation became more serious.

'As you well know, I am a wealthy man and I am almost entirely dedicated to the pursuit of money matters. I am even known to carry mint leaves in my wallet as they are reputed to attract money. Can you believe that? I own estates, properties and shipbuilding here, commerce there. Is there no end to my collection, you may ask? My only other dedication is to the welfare of my family.'

Sir Alan looked down and brushed an imaginary speck of dust from his chair before raising his head once more and regarding James frankly and steadily.

'If you will reconsider your move to Ireland and remain in London, James, I promise to introduce you to the highest echelons of our society. Without doubt you will become a celebrity man-midwife sought by the wealthy, the high and the mighty, and my darling Catherine would be more affordable to your ever expanding purse.'

Sir Alan searched out a response from James's impassive face, and finding none there continued, 'Of course if London is not to your liking, I should tell you that my cousin, the Earl of Drumaline, has a large estate not far from Dublin's Pale. So if you decide that London is not for you it may just be that you come to know more of Catherine as she holidays there at least once a year.'

As James made to reply, Sir Alan raised his hand to silence him, 'Not a word about our conversation, my friend, it is just between us. No reply is needed.' Sir Alan slid his hand into a waistcoat pocket and withdrew a gold case emblazoned with the Cavendish family crest.

'Snuff?' he enquired, putting a definite end to that conversation. 'I have here the highest quality Virginian tobacco ground up and passed through the finest sieve. No oil or flavouring added, just pure Virginian sunlight,' he said, tapping the box to loosen and gather up the powder. He offered the snuffbox to James who shook his head imperceptibly.

'Thank you. I have never taken it up.'

Sir Alan flicked the lid open and placed a couple of pinches of the precious powder at the base of his thumb.

Two profound snorts later, the snuff was deep in his nostrils.

'Ah,' he started, then sneezed massively and, eyes watering, hurriedly pulled out a large, colourful silk handkerchief from another pocket.

'Ah,' he said again once the convulsive expulsions of air had passed, a beatific gaze covering his face.

'Now you know why the Pope endeavoured to ban snuff-taking and threatened to excommunicate all who used the demon powder,' said Sir Alan. 'He knew that sneezing and conjugal ecstasies were all too similar!' He laughed delightedly, slapping his knee in emphasis, his good cheer following the sunlight around the room.

James stood in the doorway, taking in the glittering scene before him as Sir Alan made his way through the guests, heading for the drinks tray held aloft by his butler, smiling at all he passed.

The sparkling jewels in the candlelit room and the loud babble of talk and laughter made James feel a little out of place, until he saw Catherine and he thought her beautiful once more. She flitted from guest to guest, eyes twinkling, lit from within, resplendent in a dark green gown with matching feathers in her hair like an exotic bird of paradise plucked from a tropical island and deposited in the Cavendish drawing room. She saw him, and smiling, beckoned him to her side.

Across the room a dark stab of jealousy penetrated deeply into the heart of a handsome, brooding spectator. He gazed on with morbid curiosity as Catherine's soft ruby lips whispered much too close to James's ear.

Edward Burlington, the Earl of Drumaline's son, would dearly love to be in James Quinn's place, to win such a beautiful prize. He breathed out loudly and walked from the room. Having his cousin Catherine as his wife would certainly make his life easier, and her dowry would pay off his gambling debts as they arose. He resolved to set his hand to wooing her more thoroughly before she became entangled with the Irishman.

As the setting sun bathed the room in the last of its golden glow, Catherine and James stood close together in the bay window.

'May I be so bold as to enquire about your gaming with Papa?'

'Billiards and then man talk, oh, and looking under skirts.'

Catherine arched her eyebrows in pretence of annoyance.

'There you go again, teasing me so! Have you settled on a dowry as yet?' she quipped.

'Yes my dear, half of the family estate in Sussex,' James bowed, took her hand and kissed it.

'Ah, so it was that kind of man talk – my father is very fond of you, Doctor Irish man-midwife.'

'And I am fond of him,' James replied.

'Perhaps we should return to our guests; I feel the eyes of the room are upon us,' she said, and James let her hand go.

As they turned, the butler arrived with an ornate silver salver balanced on his arm, its surface strewn with an array of snuffboxes. 'Should we be bold and try some snuff, James?'

Catherine turned to him once more, enquiring humorously, 'I am told that snuff sneezing is so pleasurable, a gift from the gods for mere mortals to share.' She smiled up at James but the laughter died in her throat as she looked over and caught the gaze of Edward, who had entered so silently that she had not heard him.

The mercury liquid raced around the curved inner surface of the mortar, living up to its quicksilver name, as James stood, feet planted on the scarred, solid wood that made up the floor of William's apothecary, and rotated the vessel to and fro.

'A night time with Venus but a lifetime with Mercury,' under his breath he quoted the passage related in numerous medical texts regarding the treatment of venereal disease.

'We will require sufficient ointment for a number of applications,' said William, frowning in concentration, thinking ahead to tomorrow's work.

James had poured a half ounce of the thick liquid into the mortar, heeding the instructions from William that the mercury be well cleansed by passing it several times through double linen. To the silver liquid he added four ounces of hog's grease and beat the substances until, under his host's tutelage, they were fully mixed.

The resulting ointment was spooned into containers of two drams, the smallest amount required for an application to an infant, while an adult required a number of the containers appropriate to their size.

'Cupid has much to answer for, this *lues venerea*, this venereal plague that besets the devotees of Venus,' William was in reflective mood, 'yet the prescriptions are simpler now than ever before. Have you ever tried the fumigation remedies used by older practitioners?'

James shook his head, eager to hear more.

'It is a difficult remedy, James. First the patient is placed in a tent, naked or in a shirt, in a heated room. At his feet a portable stove glowing with the heat of hot embers on which pinches of cinnabar mercury are thrown from time to time. The fumigation continues until the patient swoons. He is then brought to bed and buried in warm blankets to make him, poor wretch, sweat profusely. The cure begins when six fumigations are completed.'

'So at that time there is severe diarrhoea and excess salivation?' enquired James.

'Indeed, just as when we apply the mercury ointment by friction. We must encourage excretion of saliva in excess of three pints each day to ensure the remedy is effective.'

'And so we apply the mercury ointment forty separate times. God bless the poor sick patient,' James replied with feeling.

'As the remedy takes hold, the nose, throat and tongue ulcerate and swell so that the speech becomes unrecognisable, the teeth and hair fall out, saliva runs constantly from the mouth, the breath stinks. Soon the entire body breaks down, but for the lucky ones a cure may be in sight.'

'And so we wonder which is preferable, the disease or the cure, but of course recovery is possible from the cure but not from the disease unless treated vigorously.'

William nodded in assent.

'But this treatment is so costly – not only once but up to forty times,' James looked to Smyley for affirmation, but he said nothing.

'How can those in lower positions in society afford the remedy?' he persisted.

'Benefactors, James, benefactors. As with all our work of this nature we spend the morning at charity and the afternoon we treat those who can pay. The fees we charge fund the entire expenses.' He turned away. 'Wherever the money comes from, James, tomorrow we spend the morning in a whore house.'

James sat in William's study that evening, reassuring in its sights of music and leather-bound books, and smelling of William's pipe so as to remind him of his own father's room, reading to refresh his understanding of the pox and the diseases that morbidly affect the privities of those given to excesses of the flesh. He beckoned to the cat, lying in his habitual pose before the fire, but the feline was having nothing to do with him and stared disdainfully at him before returning to sleep.

How strange, thought James, that Apollo – the God of healing – should curse a simple shepherd named Syphilus with the venereal disease associated with his name.

Syphilis. The great pox. The whore's pox. The worst disease of any kind to befall mankind, from which countless people suffer and die most horribly.

He ran a hand across his face wearily, pausing to shut his eyes briefly and touch them with his cool fingertips, as if doing so would remove the puffed vestiges of sleep deprivation from them, before reading on.

'You must see to it that you treat my pimps,' the Madam said to James, 'else they will not be fit to act as guardians for the girls. Many of them are beaten or otherwise badly treated by their customers, and are often in need of a strong man to come and rescue them.' She smiled and showed a set of rotting teeth.

Noticing that James had seen them, she clamped her mouth shut and sniffed, leading him to a back room in which he could commence his treatments.

'It is a shame that Dr Smyley has been called away to a woman in labour. I hope you will do your work as well as him.' And with that she left him, looking pointedly at him over her shoulder.

James looked around the room, desolation settling around him. It was shabby and ill lit, in contrast to the entrance of the house and main receiving room with its convivial atmosphere of velvet drapery and matching chairs.

The customers would not be so happy to pay for their pleasure if they had been led to this poor room, dust gathering under the broken furniture that sat in the corners gloomily, the unhappy losers in fights or other rough use.

He sat down on one of the seats, dust billowing as his weight settled and he coughed as it caught in his throat. A few minutes later, a hefty fellow with red whiskers entered the room slowly, his walk painful and difficult for all to see.

James rose from the chair.

'It's the gleet, Sir. God help me, the gleet,' moaned the pimp, and undid his breeches, pushing them to the floor where they puddled in the dust.

James knelt and inspected the man's yard, so painful, red and inflamed it had shrunk to a mere couple of inches as if endeavouring to retreat into the body itself to find comfort there.

Thick fetid purulent matter oozed from the water passage, which was ulcerated at its mouth. Nearby, the stones in their protective bag were inflamed and swollen so that at James's most delicate touch the pimp bellowed in pain.

'The piss comes forth hot and sharp like broken shards from a gin bottle, and the stones are like hot iron beaten on the anvil in the smithy's pen,' he gasped aloud, and cursed the whore he had ravaged as the devil's very own bitch.

As James knelt before the man, he felt like crushing his tender bag, squeezing hard, to inflict the pain that he knew the pimp had inflicted on others. 'At first you must drink many pints of ass's milk to cool the water in the kidneys before it flows through the yard. The cooling milk will also restore balance to the humours depleted by the disease of the privy member and stones. On the morrow, Madam will prepare an infusion to my instructions. Here, I will write the prescription for her.'

14

To take away a bruise
Boil a handful of bran in fresh water. Add to this ten
leaves of the comfrey and a good sprinkling of parsley.
Leave in the pot until most of the water is gone. Take
the pot off the fire, put the mixture in a jar and stir until
you have a paste. Apply to the bruise as hot as can be
tolerated.

Quinn Household Recipes and Remedies Book

The second pimp waiting outside the treatment room
blanched and shuffled from foot to foot in sympathy while
his friend roared in agony on the other side of the door.

He looked on worriedly as his red-haired companion
was led from the room, whimpering all the while, by his
devil's whore. He took a deep breath and entered.

A deep firm ulcer invaded the galea, the soldier's helmet
at the tip of his yard. The ulcer was the size of a medium
button and was free of hurt. Nearby, where legs met the
body, there were large buboes, hard rubbery painless lumps.

The pimp was proud of the hero's stamp on his yard, but
bitter and woeful when James reached for the mercury
ointment and ordered him to strip for a friction application.

'Can I have it hidden in chocolate like the gentry? The bastards sit in their parlours stuffing their faces with mercury while their stupid wives don't know that their rich dung-gate husbands are rotting with pox from young whores.'

James listened to the pimp rant on as he applied the ointment and was glad when he had left the room.

He was roused by a timid knock at the door, and as he opened it in answer he stood back, aghast. The once pretty young woman who stood at the door was a sad sight, and James's heart went out to her.

'Who did this to you?' he asked softly, leading her into the room.

'You just saw him,' she replied, 'the last one in here.'

Seeing James's face turn stony, she quickly countered, 'but he does mind me, honest he does. I'd be much worse off without him,' she touched his sleeve, beseechingly, trying to get him to understand the way things were in her world.

'What is your name?' he asked quietly, shamed into silence at the thought that there were women who lived like this.

'Molly.'

'Molly,' he replied, taking her face in his hand, turning it, seeing the rainbow bruising on her temples even in the poor light of the room – black, brown, blue, green, purple, pink. He saw her misshapen nose, taking the symmetry from her face, and he wanted to pull her to him and make her hurt better. He felt like weeping and then exacting revenge, in that order.

'Well, Molly, how can I help you today?'

She complained of fever, aches in the head and a bad rash, so bad nobody would hire her frail body.

'I need you to take off your gown, Molly, so I can see your rash better.'

She had no shame about disrobing in front of him, and as the fabric slid from her body he saw the angry rash, red and patchy, dispersed all over her body, her belly, chest and back bearing the brunt of the irritation.

When she had dressed again, James opened her mouth and through the gaps where teeth once sat he could plainly see elongated ulcers on the roof of her mouth tracking downwards to the back of her throat. Her hair had become thin and wispy, as strands came away in handfuls. James would need every last jar of mercury ointment to treat Molly's pox.

James Quinn's legs moved in his sleep, as in his dream he hurried to keep pace with Avril. She was just in front of him; he could nearly reach out to touch her. She wore the hooded black mantua as she had that day at Notre Dame.

'Avril!' he called, but she did not stop.

He hurried on.

'Avril!'

He ran faster, this time catching up with her, placing his hand on her cloaked shoulder. 'Avril, did you not hear me?' he asked, smiling.

'I did not,' she said, and pulled down her hood and turned to face him. Strands of her golden blonde hair came away in wisps from her scalp, and James looked on, horrified, unable to pull his eyes away from her.

She smiled at him, laughing, and through the gaps where teeth once sat he could plainly see elongated ulcers on the roof of her mouth tracking downwards to the back of her throat.

'Avril,' he said, taking her face in his hand, turning it, seeing the rainbow bruising on her temples, black, brown, blue, green, purple, pink. He saw her misshapen nose, taking the symmetry from her face.

'He does mind me, honest he does. I'd be much worse off without him,' she touched his sleeve, beseechingly.

'Avril,' the words dried in his mouth and his voice broke as he spoke her name. She pulled at the ribbon on the mantua and it fell to the street, landing like a black crow.

She had no shame about disrobing in front of him, and as the fabric slid from her body he saw the angry rash, red and patchy, dispersed all over her body, her belly, chest and back bearing the brunt of the irritation.

'Avril!' James cried, and she smiled her toothless smile.

James Quinn sat up in the bed, sheets tangled around his legs, and tried to slow his breathing. He ran his arm across his forehead, cold beads of sweat lodging there.

He left his bed, lit the candle, pulled on his shirt and sat down to write to Andre.

Paris, 10 May 1741

James,
My dear friend.

How good it was to see you letter arrive and read of your man-midwifery adventures in London.

Your William Smyley seems to have taught you much! We were possibly naive to think that the Gregoires had filled our heads with so much knowledge that we had no more to learn!

I am more than glad, also, to know that you are in such high spirits. I knew there was something sadly amiss when we first met in Paris. I have never really said this, but I am honoured that you could share your sad tale of your lost love Marguerite with me. You are a very brave man, not only to carry on with your life, but to do something worthy with it. I am proud to call myself your friend.

I know how hard you have battled with your emotions urging you on to drown your feelings with drink, but you have resisted and I am proud of you. I hope that you still are as strong as you have been. Be strong, James, be brave.

So, you are to return to Ireland next month? I hope your son Daniel is well?

All is well in Paris, indeed I have come up in the world somewhat. I met with the angel that is Avril shortly after you and I saw to it that she left her place of work and took to a much more respectable house – of ill-repute! Ha!

However, the place where she now works as the Head of the House, or Madam if we are to be more vulgar, is filled with gentlemen of discerning tastes and purses fatter than themselves. More on that in a moment.

Shortly after I met up with Avril again she agreed to be my wife. There is no other woman for me now, James, believe me, my wandering eye is stuck firmly in its socket. I fell in love with her the day you and I saw her outside the coffee house, sitting with her friends, brighter than the shining sun that afternoon.

In fact, we are soon to be parents! I am so delighted I cannot put my joy into words! Avril's pregnancy progresses well and she glows even more than usual.

Now, back to what I so briefly mentioned before. The House – where I tend to the medical needs of the girls – counts members of government and royalty, no less, as clientele. One such a gentleman mentioned a small, new town that is being built in America, in the state of Louisiana. It is called New Orleans, and is named for Phillipe II, Duc d'Orleans, one-time Regent of France.

That gentleman suggested – having told me of his visit there, and it sounds wondrous! Hot and sunny – that Avril and I may *think of opening an establishment similar to the one that we work at here, as there is no such service currently available to cater for the higher class of gentleman.*

I must admit, we are both sorely tempted, as life in Paris continues in the same way and we are eager for a fresh challenge. Due to our social standing – me as a man-midwife and her as an ugly word many people would use – our union is not looked on kindly and many doors have been closed to us through prejudice and for our daring to challenge the perception of class.

In New Orleans, Avril would be Head of the House, and part of my work as a surgeon and man-midwife will be to tend to the medical needs of the girls working there, while no doubt gaining more clients from among those that pass through the doors. Rich men will do, as I would like to provide well for my family!

We must wait until after the baby is born, of course, as I would not allow such an arduous journey by sea for my love in her condition. Oh, but our baby will be beautiful, do you not think? As long as he or she is not big, dark and hairy like me! And he or she must have a life away from the gossip-mongers of Paris and not have a life tainted just because his or her mother and father decided to fall in love despite their opposite status imposed by a fickle society.

But James, on our way we can stop to visit you in Dublin – what do you think? I would very much like to meet all the people I have come to know so well through your reminisces of them and I would relish the chance to talk face to face rather than through the written word.

So write soon to let me know what you think. I look forward greatly to hearing from you again as you continue in your quest.

I hope we shall be reunited some day very soon.

Your true friend,
Andre.

Sir Hans Sloane, the guest speaker and founding member of the Foundling Hospital in London, called his guests to attention at the art exhibition held to raise funds for the cause so close to his heart. He held up his hand for quiet, and smiling, began.

'My dear benefactors and patrons. On behalf of our president, the Duke of Bedford, and the other members of the governing body, I welcome you most heartily to London's Foundling Hospital.

'We reside here in temporary accommodation at Hatton Gardens, where we are fitted up, furnished and provided with proper officers, servants and wet and dry nurses. Meanwhile we await the building of our new institution at Lamb's Conduit Fields on grounds in Bloomsbury, purchased at great reduction from the Earl of Salisbury.

'The benefactor who first proposed this establishment does not wish any plaudits. However, you all know the man who sought support for this most worthy cause. He proposed a subscription, and over the past twenty years collected signatures to petition a charter from our glorious King. That charter was granted by His Majesty George II, in October 1739.

'That same benefactor, Captain Thomas Coram, was deeply moved by the sight of dead babies murdered and thrown upon dung hills like so many discarded slops and rubbish around this city. Their tiny bodies unloved and covered in mire.'

He cleared his throat and James saw that Catherine was weeping softly.

'I will explain. Unwanted infants or those born out of wedlock and regarded as morally degraded are murdered at birth or left exposed to perish in the streets. Those who are not abandoned are sold to persons in the lower orders and blinded, maimed or distorted in their limbs in order to move pity and compassion, and become instruments of gain to those self-same vile merciless wretches and be raised as beggars.

'It is reprehensible, but true, that more than one thousand infants are abandoned each year or thrown on the mercies of the London parishes, who cannot deal with the task. Some unfortunates are left at workhouse doors, where only one of every ten infants who enter will survive.'

The speaker paused once more and James passed Catherine a handkerchief.

'London fails miserably to provide welfare for those in need. My own researches show that in our great capital city, the pride of our nation, only one in four children are still alive by their fifth year.

'On Lady's Day this very year, the first foundlings were admitted to our Foundling Hospital. I earnestly request your further voluntary contributions to provide due and proper care for those infants, and all those who are yet to arrive, in the knowledge that you are charitable and well-disposed persons.

'As some recompense for your favours, we have arranged a body of artwork for you to fill the senses. Now my final, pleasant duty is to declare this exhibition officially open. Shake out your purses, ladies and gentlemen, for this is the work of the Lord!'

Thunderous applause greeted him, and ladies around the room were seen dabbing at their eyes with lace handkerchiefs. Catherine was not the only one to have her heart touched by the speech.

When the applause waned, the string quartet nestled by the stairwell tuned up and soon the lively passages from Handel's 'Ode for St Cecilia's Day' danced through the building.

15

To ease the painful menses

Make a tea by boiling the leaves of raspberry in a pot of fresh water (a goodly handful of these should suffice). Strain the leaves from the water and leave until cool enough to drink. You may add sugar and ginger to sweeten and flavour, and drink as often as is needed.

Quinn Household Recipes and Remedies Book

James and Catherine moved from the spacious hallway to view the exhibits, both silent at the thought of unloved babies and children treated so.

'James, this is Captain Coram the great man, an acquaintance of my father, of course.' Catherine pointed at the painting of the white-haired captain who sat resplendent in his fine clothing and greatcoat surrounded by seafaring images, a globe at his feet.

'A portrait of a great man,' said James as he bent forward to read from the sign close by. '"A portrait of Captain Thomas Coram donated to the London Foundling Hospital by William Hogarth, 1740." Your father's acquaintance also?' he enquired light-heartedly.

'Do you remember the portrait of father holding a brace of pheasants in the gaming room? Painted by William and a gift to my father in return for Lord only knows what.'

James nodded, unsurprised, and they wandered on.

'Oh, James, one of my favourites!'

James admired the painting of three milkmaids dancing to a tune played by a fiddler with a peg leg.

'It's so full of music, life and gaiety,' she breathed contentedly, smiling at the image.

'Somewhat like your own life, I dare say – I think I could fall for you as simple country lass, just in from the milking parlour.'

'And I could see you stomping around on a peg leg!' she retorted.

'Francis Hayman,' James read aloud.

'He decorated the dinner boxes in the New Spring Gardens at Vauxhall. And Francis is friendly with the actress Peg Woffington and her friend the actor David Garrick because he painted stage sets in the Drury Lane Theatre.'

Catherine moved away.

'Do hurry on please, James, and admire this maid you accompany rather than those wenches in oil paints.' He was taken aback at her tone, but followed and was rewarded with a grin.

'Your life laid out for all to see,' Catherine declared impishly, and motioned to the eight large pictures hanging there.

'"A Rake's Progress" by William Hogarth – the set of paintings tells the story of Tom Rakewell, son of a rich merchant who came to live in London. Sadly he fell into a life of debauchery, landing up in prison and eventually Bedlam, home for the insane,' she said. 'I will rest a while to allow you to recall your past deeds.'

Catherine looked pale on James's return but fended off his enquiries with a dismissive wave of her hand and a small, tight smile.

'Perhaps we should return to our carriage,' he said, worried for her now, and led Catherine towards the entrance hall.

They stopped at a large sketch depicting the proposed drawings for the new Foundling Hospital building; two wings and a chapel surrounding a central court in its own grounds surrounded by walls with gracious entrance gates, equipped to house four hundred children from the age of three years onwards. The younger foundlings would be received there as infants but then sent to the country, far away from the foul air of the city during their early years.

Beside the sketch was a list of benefactors whose kindness and charity would bring the hospital to completion. James spied a familiar name.

'Sir Alan Cavendish. I understood your father's main intent was the accumulation, not the disposal of wealth,' he quipped.

'A person is not always as you perceive them,' she replied a little distantly.

Close to the entrance, a nurse stood beside a cot.

'A deserted foundling of our fair city,' read the notice at the infant's head.

James felt a shooting pain through his heart as he thought of his son. Had he not deserted him? It was just as well he was on his way home soon. He would show Daniel that his father's heart would be held in his small hands, and that his father's life was his.

As the carriage trundled along, Catherine became paler still, and her hand fell to her belly.

'Catherine, you must tell me, have I done something to offend you? Or are you unwell?'

She shook her head, unwilling to answer him.

'Catherine?' he asked again, softly.

'Oh James, it is nothing! A woman's life, James, it is a woman's life to be this way,' she snapped and turned her head away from him.

Ah, now he understood.

'Your courses have appeared, is that it? Thank God, I was worried about you, and I thought you were cross at me for something I had done.'

'Hush, James.'

He held her hand for the remainder home, her ashen face unhappy.

'Could we fetch some vinegar from the kitchen?' James enquired once they were inside her father's house.

She looked at him quizzically, eyebrow raised.

'If we boil a piece of strong sea sponge in vinegar we can lay it on the affected parts to good effect, or so the old wives tales tell us. Or a fumigation of vinegar with the smoke of burnt frogs or mule's hoof received while sitting on a close stool is most efficacious.'

'You may close the door quietly on your way out.' Catherine was not amused.

He sat at the piano and stumbled over some notes as she looked on tearfully.

'I enjoyed our time together today, James.'

'As did I,' he replied, looking up from the piano. He saw her eyes brimming and her determination not to let the tears spill over, her lashes wet. He got up and crossed the room to be with her.

'It will be a long time until September when we meet again.' As she looked at him he saw her lower lip tremble a little, and she blinked furiously, annoyed with herself; she would not cry. He took her hands, which were ice cold, and rubbed them within his own to warm them and hopefully return the bloom to her cheeks.

'I will be waiting at the dock to take you in my arms when your ship is due and we can travel together to your uncle's estate. You are set to holiday for the month, so maybe you could make a tiny space in your calendar to be with me. And in the meanwhile, write to me and I will reply to every letter, no matter how busy I am.'

As she smiled bravely for him, her tears fell, stronger than her restraint. He cupped her face in his hands and kissed her on the brow, brushing away a stray hair and gently wiping the tears that silvered her cheeks with their descent. He kissed his finger then put it to her lips and took her into his arms.

She watched from the window until his carriage disappeared from view, then sat at the piano and poured her heart out onto the keys.

'I cannot thank you enough, William. Words can't express how much I am in your debt,' James shook his hand, looking him in the eye.

'Now James, you were of great assistance to me and to Eupham, and you must write and tell me how you are faring in Dublin.'

'And you must come and visit, should you get the chance.'

'Here, James, I have made some food for you for your voyage. You must keep your strength up to meet your son again after so long away, little soul.' Eupham smiled up at him and pressed the neatly wrapped package into his hands. 'Do not worry about returning the linen, our household sometimes seems to groan under the weight of it!'

He bent down to embrace her.

'Thank you, Eupham, for everything – you have been like a mother to me, and a very good friend.'

'Oh, away with you!' she replied, but her lace cap bobbed atop her curls and he could tell she was pleased.

'Let us know how you get on, won't you James,' she continued, 'and you are more than welcome in our home any time, isn't that so William?'

'It is indeed, dear. It is indeed. Now James, I have my own parting gift for you, so you may remember us.'

James was dismayed.

'But I have nothing for you, and surely it is me who should be giving you something after your many kindnesses to me.'

'Now, James, take this,' William passed a large parcel to him. 'Open it on your journey back, and perhaps on your return to Ireland let us know all your news. That will be thanks enough.'

James left his hosts standing at their door, waving him off. He settled back into the carriage that was taking him to the port and his waiting ship. As they sped on, he saw a group of small urchins playing their favourite game, little faces smeared with grime which made their teeth shine whitely.

'London Bridge is falling down, falling down, falling down. London Bridge is falling down, my fair lady.'

They laughed in delight and the strains of their childish voices followed the carriage for a while before being lost to his ears.

He sat back and thought of Catherine.

On his arrival at the port, James looked on in awe. It was indeed as busy as William had said it would be, and many types of boat pitched and rolled on the swell. He felt the familiar queasiness hit him and sweat stood on his forehead.

He hated journeys by sea with a vengeance. The two-masted craft that stood at the quay waiting to carry him home did little to raise his spirits.

In his tiny cabin, the smell of tar and the malodour of the latrine close by were overpowering. Soon he knew he would be like countless London women who puked their guts up during pregnancy.

He made his way out on deck to take some air and, he hoped, ease his roiling stomach. He breathed deeply again and wiped his sweaty forehead with a hand that was starting to tingle. The words of Hippocrates, the physician of ancient Greece, reverberated around his head: 'A vomit is but a bad hiccup.'

As the sweat started to flow freely, an impending sense of dread came upon him. He ran to the rail and leaned over as the contents of his stomach, Eupham's fine breakfast of cheese and eggs, hit the Thames with force and swam on the water, greasy and half digested.

He laid his head on the rail, knowing full well that this would be just the first of many episodes over the following days, as the boat wallowed on the high seas. He spat into the heaving water.

James returned and lay in desolation on the mean bunk in his dingy cabin until he felt a rumble in his fundament that arrived without the blessing of a purge. To distract himself from his sickness, he opened William's gift and gasped. The man-midwife had given him a pannier containing obstetric forceps and other instruments which would be invaluable to him in his work.

James smiled and then moaned, putting his arm over his eyes, swaying with the movement of the boat, Eupham's food parcel laying discarded on the floor, never to be eaten.

16

To aid the sleep of children
Boil enough fresh water to fill a cup and sprinkle on the top of it a handful of dried chamomile flowers. Leave in the pot for a little and then remove from the fire. Let it stand to cool, strain it into the cup and add some honey to taste. This will bring sleep to the child and is also excellent for troubles and hurts caused by the teeth coming through.

Quinn Household Recipes and Remedies Book

DUBLIN, 1741-1742

James Quinn waited impatiently for Peg to open the door to him.

'I'm coming, I'm coming,' she called, and fumbled with the heavy key, lock and latch to let him in.

'Peg! How good it is to see you!' he dashed into the hall and took her in his arms, twirling her around, her hair falling loose around her shoulders.

'Why, James – Doctor James, should I say – it is good to

see you too, but now do me the favour of returning me to the ground!'

He laughed at her and put her down, hugging her tight. 'Peg, it is so good to be home. And now I must go and see Daniel,' and he bounded away, taking the stairs two at a time.

'James! He is asleep this long time. Come back down here and be reasonable.'

'Peg, it has been too long. I have waited so long to see my boy and I have a present for him too.'

'Even so, come on down and you can look in on him later and meet him properly tomorrow, give him his gift, when he has had his rest. You look like you could do with yours too, I think.'

He made his way down the stairs again, sighing, head down. She laughed out loud.

'What? What is so funny, Peg?'

'I see that look on your son's face often, when he has spied something and set his little heart on it, only for it to be taken away when it is within his grasp. Come, stand by me. Let me look at you,' and she took him by the hand and led him into the light.

She took his face in her hands and nodded, pleased at what she saw there.

'You are still as handsome as ever. I bet you set the London ladies' hearts all aflutter. Your eyes shine, and you look better than I have seen you in this long time. Since Marguerite,' she stopped.

'Peg,' he said tenderly, 'I am over my dark time, but never my love for Marguerite.' He took her hands in his, holding them softly, looking into her eyes.

'And glad I am to see it. But now, I know you are tired and I must lock the door. You should go to bed.'

James smiled at her bossy tone; some things never changed. She locked and latched the door, put the key back in her pocket, and turned to look at him.

'Well now, you do look all done in. Will you have a hot drink? No? Straight to bed for you then and you can see Daniel in the morning. Your bed is all ready for you.'

'But Peg, I want to see him now.'

'Leave him sleep and see him tomorrow.'

'Peg, it is too long since I have seen him. I have waited long enough.'

'Well then,' she laughed, 'do what you will, but please try not to wake him. All the excitement of your homecoming has tired him out these past few days and he has not been himself,' she looked pointedly at him.

'You can meet Carissa tomorrow, she too is asleep. And I will leave some warm milk for you before turning in myself.'

'I'm fine, Peg, I really don't want any.'

'You'll have some milk, James, and it will make you feel better and sleep soundly. Now goodnight to you.'

James paused in his ascent of the stairs and looked down at her through a gap in the turned wood of the banisters. 'Peg?'

'Yes James?' she replied and turned to look up at him.

'It is good to see you, even if you will insist on treating me as no older than a child of Daniel's age.' He smiled at her retreating back as she went to the kitchen to make his drink.

James Quinn pushed the door open, and tiptoed into the room where his son slept. He stood for a while and gazed down at the boy's small body, wrapped up in blankets.

He watched as Daniel's breath pushed his ribcage up and down. The child's thumb was in his mouth, a small blanket in the same hand, his lashes caressing his cheeks softly.

James sat on the bed and soon his breath was in rhythm with his son's. He brushed the boy's hair across his forehead with his hand, and bent down to kiss him, smelling sleep and warmth on him.

He became lost in thought as his eyes roamed around the room, seeing the shapes of toys and books, a small chair and bedside table, before kissing his son once more and making his way to his own slumber.

Sometime in the night James was woken and he sat up in bed, in his tiredness thinking he was still at the Smyley's home, being called out to a woman in childbirth. As he reached for his shirt he realised where he was and sat back.

He could hear Daniel crying and the soft voice of a woman as she settled him. Carissa, he thought, as his sleep-fuddled brain slowly offered her name up to him. James lay back down and heard the familiar Irish words of the 'Connemara Lullaby' being sung to his son to help him back to sleep. His own mother had sung this often to him, and he was transported back to his childhood bed in Galway, with her sweet voice lulling away whatever had woken him, words luring back sleep, beckoning dreams. He sighed and rolled over.

'*Codladh sámh a leanbh.* Go to sleep, my baby, your daddy's coming home. He caught some silver herring, for you and me alone. Go to sleep my baby, the stars are in the sky. No more he'll go a-wandering. For he loves us, you and I.'

James watched from the door of the kitchen as the two women sat with the boy, sunlight streaming in, alighting on the plates that sat on the scrubbed table.

'Now, Daniel,' Peg was saying, 'if you are a good boy and eat up all of your food we shall go and wake your daddy, for it is time he was up!'

'Yes, Peg,' Daniel nodded sagely, 'not good to be sleeping. Playing instead!' and he swung his legs excitedly at the thought of all the things he might do and adventures he might have that day. 'See a cat?' he enquired.

'Good boy, Daniel. We will get Daddy and go for a walk, and maybe we will see a cat, or perhaps a dog or a horse,' Carissa said.

James grinned, eager to go to his son, but happy for the moment taking in the breakfasting trio.

Peg passed some bread, thickly spread with butter, to Daniel, which he promptly stuffed in his mouth in his eagerness to be off.

'Now Daniel, where are your manners? We do not put a whole piece of bread in our mouth in this house!' Peg chided him gently.

'Auntie Lynch's house?' he enquired, tripping over her name, and the women laughed.

'Later, my lovely, we will go for tea and cake. After our walk.'

'Cake!' squealed the boy, clapping his hands in delight.

James looked at Carissa. He had seen her last at her father's funeral – poor Liam O'Flaherty. He saw how time had changed her from the sad, heartbroken youngster to the attractive woman that sat before him now. Carissa was talking to Daniel, handing him a cup of milk and wiping off the creamy moustache that it left on his lip tenderly with her thumb. James smiled as Carissa pushed some dark, unruly curls behind her ear.

'Good morning,' he said from the door, and three faces met his. Carissa kept hold of Daniel's hand in her slight one, her pretty face smiling. Peg rose from the table.

'Why James, come and join us, there is fresh tea. And here is your boy waiting patiently to see you.'

Seated at the table, the small boy looked up at the tall man, with his happy face and twinkling eyes. And he was shy suddenly and didn't know this man who was his daddy. He clambered onto Carissa's lap and put his head on her shoulder, looking up at his daddy, thumb firmly in his mouth.

The man who was his daddy sat down beside them and started to talk to Carissa, saying hello, and how are you.

'And now,' James said, turning to him, 'Daniel, I am so glad to see you, I have missed you very much and am very happy to be home,' he smiled. 'Will you come for a cuddle, for I have long waited to feel my arms around you.' And he held his arms out to him.

The little boy's face crumpled, his eyes filled with tears, his lip trembled. There was complete silence. And then Daniel cried from deep within, howling, the tears falling from his brown eyes.

Peg and James sat frozen, dismayed, as Carissa gathered the child more tightly into her arms, cooing to him and telling him that here was his daddy home and that they would be good friends and that everything would be just fine.

'Daniel, what is wrong my little love?' asked Peg when the storm of weeping subsided. Daniel looked at James and back to Peg from the safety of Carissa's embrace. James stood, pushed his chair back and knelt before the small boy.

'Daniel,' he said, and took his son's hand in his own, 'we have much to learn about each other, you and I. And it may take a little time, but we have lots of it, for I am home for good now. What's more, I have brought you a present all the way from London.'

The boy's face brightened.

'Now, Daniel. I looked into your room last night when you were fast asleep, but I didn't get to see all your toys and books because of the dark. I hear you have a spinning top from Galway? Shall we go and see it?'

Daniel wriggled out of Carissa's lap, took his daddy's hand and led him out of the room.

'Have you my present?' came the childish voice. The boy's voice echoed down the hall to them, James's reply lost as they climbed the stairs, hand in hand.

Peg sighed with relief, 'That went as well as could be expected, I suppose. From small, slow beginnings come great things, you wait and see, Carissa,' she said. 'Carissa?'

But Carissa was lost in thought as she remembered the terrible day James Quinn had come to their home, the day her father was laid out cold and stiff, her mother laying down weeping, and how she never wanted him to leave. Now, unexpectedly, she felt the same way.

'Cake soon, Daddy?' Daniel asked his father as they walked to St Anne's churchyard under the cheerful, sunny Dublin skies.

'Cake soon, Daniel,' said James, smiling down at him. 'At Aunt and Uncle Lynch's house, just around the corner.'

'She does let me help. I am a good helper,' Daniel told him solemnly.

'Yes, my boy, I am sure you are.'

James was distracted and unhappy, not sure how he would feel when he reached Marguerite's grave. He remembered his last time at the church, and blushed as he recalled his behaviour.

Peg noticed James's discomfort and guessed its reason, though she had never told him of his brandy-soaked confession to her, and she took Daniel's hand and walked with him and Carissa. James wandered on alone, lonely for

Marguerite and feeling the ongoing loss of her in his life so deeply that it hurt.

The graveyard was peaceful and quiet, with birdsong and a soft wind moving through the yew trees, disturbing their upright finery only a little. As James walked up to Marguerite's grave, a butterfly flew past, a bright reminder of life among the angels and granite headstones of the dead.

'Hello Marguerite, my darling, I am sorry that it has been so long,' he whispered and knelt down, running his fingers over the inscription on her headstone, his vision obscured by tears.

'Sacred to the memory of much beloved Marguerite Quinn, who departed this life on the 14th day of July 1738 aged 23 years.'

He had been too distraught to come up with the words; his father and Marguerite's had told the stonemason what to inscribe. And then the memories of her and how she would never be here again with him, to hold him and love him, talk with him, share Daniel with him, overcame James again and tears rolled down his cheeks. He bent his shoulders and wept for the woman he loved.

'Why is Daddy crying?' James heard a small voice ask Carissa.

'He misses your mother, my dote, and he is feeling very sad,' she said with a catch in her voice. Daniel held out his hand to Carissa, and Peg stood back to let James grieve. They walked away quietly, but he did not hear them anyway.

'Are you still crying?' Daniel asked a little later, pulling at his father's sleeve, worry written all over his face. 'Why are you crying? Do you miss Mummy? I did never see her. Did you hurt your own self Daddy? A nice cup of milk makes you better.' The small boy held out his arm and wiped his sleeve over his father's wet cheeks.

James smiled at Daniel through his tears.

'Here,' said his small son, and handed him a bedraggled posy of wildflowers that he had picked. 'For Mummy in Heaven. And the angels. They like pretty flowers. I did pick them my own self. But Carissa helped me. Don't cry, my daddy.'

James looked at Marguerite's living memory and wiped his eyes, watching as Daniel laid the tiny bouquet on her grave.

'What is that furry one, Daddy? Daniel asked, pointing to the flowers.

'Why, that is a very special one, Daniel. It is called a dandelion and the furry part is the lion's mane, or other people call it a clock.'

Daniel looked on, bewildered.

James picked the dandelion up in his hand and blew on it, the tiny white feathers making their way up into the sky. 'You see these, Daniel, flying towards the sun?'

Daniel nodded.

'These are called wishes. You know what a wish is? When you want something? Well, you blow here,' and he showed his small son where to blow, 'and the wish goes up and up, and then you can whisper the thing that you want after it and it will carry it away and your wish will come true. Would you like to have a go?'

Daniel took the dandelion out of his father's hand, and blew furiously on it, white down scattering and dancing above his head. He scratched his nose as the nap tickled his upper lip on its ascent.

'I did wish, Daddy. For you to be not crying no more.'

James got up from his knees and held his son tightly, then released him and took his hand in his own as Peg and Carissa came to stand with them.

'No more tears,' he told Daniel, 'just happy stories about your mother that I will tell you any time you like, for she was strong and beautiful and brave. She loved you very much and would not want us to cry for her.'

Then they were walking to the Lynches' home on Coote Lane, Carissa ahead with Daniel, James and Peg behind.

'Thank you for tending to Marguerite's grave while I was away, Peg; it is nice to know that she has been cared for as well as Daniel has. I cannot thank you enough for both.'

Peg stopped and looked at him.

'Caring for Daniel has been a real pleasure for Carissa and myself. But it is she alone who has been tending to Marguerite's grave.'

James looked intently as Carissa went on with Daniel, hand-in-hand, singing as they went.

17

To stop bugs and insects from feasting upon roses
Small insects and other crawling ones like to feast upon
roses, eating the blooms and destroying them. For the
one, plant parsley in between the roses. For the other,
sprinkle sugar on which they will feed instead.

Quinn Household Recipes and Remedies Book

'He loves it here, Aunt Lynch. Thank you for everything.'

Sarah Lynch sat with James and they watched Daniel play
hide-and-seek with Peg in the small, rose-covered garden at
the back of their house.

She took his hand and smiled at Daniel's childish laughter
ringing out.

'It has been a joy,' she replied, 'like having a little piece of
Marguerite here with us still.'

He squeezed her hand.

Upstairs, Carissa sat with her sister Aileen, who had
travelled with her from Galway and now worked for Sarah
and Bernard Lynch.

'He's nice. Good-looking too,' Aileen said playfully.

'Who's that?' replied Carissa, but her blush gave her away.

'I knew it! You like him!' Aileen got off the bed on which they were both sitting and danced around the room.

'Aileen!'

'Here comes a grand fellow to sweep you off your feet and dance you round and round in your fine gown. May I?' she enquired, bowed before her sister, hand outstretched. Carissa took it laughingly and danced with her sister, until they collapsed on the bed in a heap of feminine exhaustion.

'Be careful,' her sister said, seriously, 'a broken heart is not an affliction you want to suffer from.'

'How would you know, Aileen?' replied Carissa, and seeing the hurt in her sister's eyes breathed out and changed the subject.

'I don't quite know what to do with him, and I feel so bad about it. First my indifference and prolonged absence and now, at the very start of trying to build up my relationship with Daniel, I don't know how to be.' James looked at the patterned rug.

'Ah James,' replied Sarah Lynch, 'be yourself. You must feel your way slowly and gently. It will take time, but you will earn his trust.' She put her hand on his arm and looked him deep in the eyes. 'Children are very trusting; he will come round, James. You must relax until he does. He will feel your emotions and take his actions from them. But do not spoil him in recompense for imagined slights, for you will ruin him – do the simple things with him, James, and all will be well. Guilt will get you nowhere.'

She saw that his eyes were glassy bright with tears.

'Daniel looks just like that when he is doing his best not to cry; his nose reddens in just the same way.'

James smiled and blew out his breath.

Daniel waved in the window to his father and great-aunt and they smiled and waved back.

'You see?' urged Sarah Lynch. 'And you know where we are if you ever need to talk. You are doing Marguerite proud, James. You have become an even finer man and will be a great father to Daniel.' She took his hand and held it. 'And now I hear my errant husband!'

'I am sorry, I was kept late with work.' He kissed his wife on her proffered cheek and said to James, 'You look well, James, time has been fair. Better to you than me, I fear, with my new paunch!' He slapped James on the back and sat as Sarah poured the tea.

'I am grateful for the time and kindness you have given Daniel while I have been away,' said James. 'Peg and Carissa too. Daniel loves it here; he told me so.'

Sarah smiled.

'Also for our house, which you have not charged us for while I have been away, thank you. But now I am back, and eager to settle up my debts. I am sorry it was not arranged before I left, but I was in no fit state.'

Sarah looked at him in understanding.

He went on, 'I wonder, Uncle Lynch, if you would be so kind as to set up a meeting with your banker for me? I would like to buy our house and pay my father-in-law back for financing my studies in Paris and London. I couldn't have done it without your help.'

'Bernard can arrange the meeting, James, but you and I need to arrange some new clothes for your meetings!' Sarah smiled at him once more and Bernard laughed as James's face fell at the thought of going to the tailor for fittings.

Dublin, 4 July 1741

My dearest Catherine,
I hope this letter finds you well and many thanks for your news from London.

How I miss our time together and the sweet notes you coax from the piano. If I close my eyes, I can see you there, fingers on the keys, picking out exquisite melodies.

I myself have been very busy since my return, getting to know Daniel – whom I am sure you will love! – and meeting up with friends and family here. Daniel turns three in ten days' time, so we are all in a state of high excitement and planning a cake, toys and books for him.

Daniel, Peg, Carissa who looks after him, and myself travelled down to Galway last week to see my family, and what a welcome we received. He was very excited to see both sets of his grandparents and my sister, his Aunt Kate, and had to bring Carissa everywhere with him – they are quite a pair – with our family dog Finn following close behind.

My mother and Daniel are firm friends and she even let him help her to make a cake. You can only imagine the chaos! He was very impressed by my father's study with its grown-up books, as he called them, but quite put out when he was not allowed to try the pipe.

Thomas Lynch sat him on his shoulders and Daniel loved sitting at such a great height, while his Grandmother Lynch clucked around and fretted about Daniel falling from that great height and hitting his head!

It felt so good to be home after all this time, and I can't wait for you to meet my family.

And now, Catherine, let me tell you a story.

Once upon a time there was a beautiful girl, and her name was Galvia. Now, she was not as beautiful as you, her eyes did not sparkle like gems, nor her curly hair caress her shoulders as yours does, but she was beautiful nonetheless.

This girl, Galvia, was a princess, and she spent her days doing royal things. But one terrible day, some say nursing a broken heart, she fell into the rushing waters of the River Corrib and was drowned. It is after the princess Galvia that Galway is named.

Fear not, Catherine, your tale is sure to have a much happier ending, and we will stand by the Corrib and perhaps think of Galvia before walking to the spot where the explorer Christopher Columbus stood before his great voyage, and go on to the fine building that is the King's Head to admire the marriage stones over the hearth there.

James's writing was interrupted when Daniel ran into his study, with Carissa in quick pursuit.

'Daddy!'

'Daniel, you can sit on my knee. I'm writing to Catherine, a lovely lady who is coming to see you and me in September.'

Carissa stood quietly, taken aback; she hadn't realised there may be a new woman in his life. Her heart thumped uncomfortably in her chest.

'Here Daniel, smell the lovely perfume on the letter she wrote to me. She might even come to live with us. Isn't that wonderful?' and he hugged his son to him.

'I am going to play again!' Daniel declared and he squirmed away as Carissa stood in the doorway, watching as James bent his head to continue writing. Then she turned and went after Daniel.

And Catherine, Barna, beautiful Barna. James looked out in the window and was lost in sweetly precious reverie.

The water babbled sweetly as James and Marguerite sat on the grass in the sun–dappled clearing in Barna Woods. They could hear the sea in the distance and the birds singing close by. Low stone walls guarded James and his love that day, and the sun shone through the ancient trees made by nature, encircling them, protecting them.

Marguerite, made languid by the heat and stillness, laid her head on James's chest and he could smell her sweetness. Her lashes swept her curved cheek and she sighed with happiness.

James tickled her gently.

'James! I'm trying to rest!'

He tickled her again, and she laughed and pushed him away playfully.

They lay down again and talked of how they would be together forever and ever, as the smell of the earth, the sea, and the sun on the trees and their skin filled the air. The beauty of it all embraced their souls and they knew they would never be the same again, filled as they were with the clarity of the depth of their emotions for each other.

He bent down to embrace her and kissed her softly.

'I love you, Marguerite.'

James Quinn sat at his desk, the candle illuminating the work laid out in front of him, the summer evening finally darkening, and read over what he had written in his journal:

Collection 1, Of Laborious Cases Delivered by Instruments, Number 1, Case 1. Attendance on Mrs Slaney on William Street near by Mercer's Hospital for the Poor, 20 July 1741.

At an early hour when all slept soundly, a note was carried to me from my friend and mentor Surgeon Laurence Stone. A woman lay undelivered and in a perilous situation. In his message he wrote that Doctor McFadden had failed to bring the case to a satisfactory end; it may be that the man had theoretical knowledge but lacked sufficient practical experience in the art of childbirth.

As the woman remained undelivered despite much effort, he determined to insert a whalebone fillet to assist delivery but failed in his attempts to introduce the instrument past the infant's face.

On later application of a vectis, the woman's internal parts were rent by the metal lever and bled profusely. No further progress being apparent, the midwives had urgently requested the attendance of my friend and mentor. They followed his advice and then sought my presence instead for the birth.

James Quinn felt the woman's pulse, which raced under his fingers. He took in her swollen face, cheeks red and feverish. Her tongue was so dry that she could not answer his gentle questions. He called for broth and sack wine for the weakened woman.

'Mrs Slaney, I am here to help bring your child into your arms. But to do that, and I need you to have no fear, I must touch you.'

The woman's eyes widened, but she nodded, and could not help stiffening as James Quinn gently inserted his forefinger into her vagina, having first greased it well with fresh butter. He hid his worry; he had not been able to feel as high up as he would have liked as she was so swollen.

'Well done,' he said. 'I need you to sleep for a little while now.'

He held her head as he gave her a mixture of Aqua Fontana spring water and syrup of meconium juice of the opium poppy, sweetened with sugar, and soon her eyes closed and the crease between her brows relaxed.

He applied a large poultice of loaf-bread and milk with hog's lard to her privities in an attempt to bring down the swelling.

Once Mrs Slaney woke, he removed the poultice and washed her. He breathed out in relief; the area had calmed down considerably.

'Midwife O'Hara, Midwife Kelly, please help me to lay Mrs Slaney on her back but with her legs over the edge of the bed. More pillows for her head,' he saw the woman settled, 'and now support a leg each.' He nodded his thanks once everything was to his satisfaction.

James Quinn inserted his finger once more, and this time was able to feel the hairy scalp of the infant low down in Mrs Slaney's pelvis. To his great relief he realised that the baby was alive as no fetid cadaverous fluid escaped past its head to run down his fingers.

Taking great care, James Quinn took the delivery forceps that William Smyley had given him and wrapped the instrument in linen so as not to panic the poor woman with the clanking sound of metal blade against metal. Keeping the blades low down and hidden, he felt again for the position of the baby's head and knew that its ears were to the sides of the mother's pelvis.

Gently dilating Mrs Slaney, he introduced the right forceps blade between his hand and the child's head, and the woman let out a piercing, pained shriek.

The midwives watched intently as they had never seen forceps before but held their silence; their trust in James bolstered by the recommendation from Surgeon Stone.

With his left hand he inserted the second long blade on the opposite side of the vagina and then tied both blades firmly together with a garter to stop them from slipping.

'Mrs Slaney,' he spoke softly to the woman on the bed, her face distressed, eyes glittering with tears, 'we are now going to try to deliver you of your child. I will need all of your help.'

The midwives held her legs and muttered calming words. James began.

'Now push,' he said.

On every push, he pulled on the forceps, their precious load held within the blades. Pulling by intervals, the child's head gradually appeared into the world, then James removed the forceps and delivered the rest of the tiny body.

The infant girl's mother let out a scream, for her child's head was squeezed into a lengthened form akin to a sugar loaf because of the over-long time spent in the birth canal. James reassured her and turned his attention to the baby once more. She was not breathing.

He took the tiny body into his hands and shook her gently. Still no breath. He rubbed spirits and an onion on her rosebud mouth and under her nose. When this failed, he opened her mouth and breathed in to her. Her indignant squalling caused both midwives to smile broadly and the new mother to cry in delight as her daughter was finally laid into her arms.

18

To get a shine on your furniture

Pare a candle of beeswax into small bits. Put these into a pot and add a cup of water. Place on the fire to boil, stirring until the mixture is thick, and take it off. Add in just a drop or two of oil of pressed lavender and stir. Put the mixture into a jar with a lid to keep it soft. Rub it onto your furniture with a fine cloth, then take another cloth and buff until it shines.

Quinn Household Recipes and Remedies Book

'We have much to do, girls, before Catherine Cavendish arrives here. What a fine name; how it rolls off the tongue. Well, by all accounts, from what James has told me, she is quite the lady, and the darling of the glittering London scene,' said Peg.

Aileen and Carissa sighed at the story she was bringing to life for them with her words and gestures, of lords and ladies, actors and actresses, poets and writers, singers and musicians.

'Will she stay here, Peg?' asked Aileen.

'No, my dear, no. She is to stay either in Meath with her father's cousins who own a sprawling estate there, or in

Clontarf Castle with her father's friends John and Dorothy Vernon.'

'It sounds like a tale you would tell Daniel at bedtime, so grand!'

Peg smiled at Aileen, 'It is no tale. And she will be here in the flesh, wearing her beautiful gowns and jewels next month.' She paused, looking at Carissa's stricken face. 'Why Carissa, what is the matter?'

'It is just that he still seems so in love with Marguerite, that's all.'

Peg reached across the table and took her hand. 'Well, he is. He always will be, after all, she is Daniel's mother. But Carissa, you cannot expect a young, vibrant man like him to shut himself off from the world forever. He cannot hold a memory at night!'

Carissa sat back, quietly, unhappy.

'They may well marry,' continued Peg, 'and wouldn't it be marvellous for Daniel to have a proper mother after all this time?'

'But Peg! What about you and me?' asked Carissa urgently. 'Will she take him away from us?'

'Carissa O'Flaherty! How can you say such a thing, of course not. Daniel will still need you to care for him and I will continue to run the house.'

Aileen looked at Carissa and knew then, for certain, that it had not been Daniel she was talking about. She felt heartsore for her sister.

'But enough chattering, girls. We will need to make a list of the things that must be done before her arrival. We need to prepare the house and clean from top to bottom and make sure to put an extra shine on all the furniture. And what kind of entertainment can we put on here in our home for someone who is used to living in London?' Peg put the heel of her hand to her forehead and rubbed it vigorously. 'Oh my, I feel a headache coming on, I swear I do. So much to do in so little time. And as for the food, what to feed her? I declare I am worn out already!'

'Peg, we will help you, won't we Carissa. Carissa?' Aileen nudged her sister, who sat gloomily, vacantly in the chair beside her.

'Of course,' she answered, and, catching Peg's disapproving look, sat up straight and arranged her unwilling mouth into her best approximation of a smile.

'Good then, that's settled, let's make a start,' and she smiled at the girls.

They rose to leave the room.

'And girls,' called Peg, 'we will all have to speak English while she is here. Daniel too.'

They groaned and left the room, while Peg sat happily among her plans.

Well then, that was that. Carissa looked at the beautiful woman standing there and she knew that all was lost. She could never compete. Never. Not if she lived to be one hundred years old.

She felt jealousy, dislike, fear, loss and envy scratch their claws across her body, one after the other, and wanted to sink to the floor and weep as they left their cruel imprints behind on her tender flesh. And then Catherine was standing before her, extending her hand, smiling, and Carissa had to shake her head to hear properly and send the feelings away.

'It is so lovely to meet you, Carissa, in person. I have heard much of you from James, but he never told me how pretty you are.'

And Carissa thought herself a fool as she blushed at the woman's kind words.

'And how good you are with Daniel and how he loves you. What a lucky man to have his son so well cared for!' She smiled at Carissa and Carissa melted as if a spell had been placed on her. She liked this Catherine. She didn't want to like her but she could see now why James loved her, and tears threatened, so she turned away and busied herself with something inconsequential as she heard the rest of the introductions being made, James proudly introducing his new heart's desire to Aileen and Peg, and their warm replies. Catherine had won them all over. All was lost.

'Carissa, dear, meet my cousin Edward and his companion Charles,' Catherine said, and Carissa turned back, smile firmly in place.

Edward inclined his head as he said his hello, but Charles was more forthcoming and grabbed her hand and kissed it saying, 'Enchanted, I'm sure,' looking deep into her eyes.

'Catherine, come now and meet the special boy in my life,' James said to her and he took her hand and led her out of the room.

'I must go, I have a shoot to attend in Clontarf,' said Edward and bowed stiffly to the rest of the group. Peg showed him out and went on into the kitchen to prepare a meal, humming a jaunty tune under her breath.

Aileen followed her, looking back to see Charles in conversation with Carissa, hanging on to her every word as if the sentences she spoke dripped with honey. She smiled.

'This is my best cat,' Daniel said to Catherine as she sat on his small bed. 'My daddy brung it from London,' and he held the wooden toy out for her closer inspection. 'I did want to sleep with it. But Carissa said no, it is too hard

Daniel.' He relayed his tale seriously and pushed the toy even nearer to Catherine.

'My, what a marvellous cat! And what a clever daddy to choose you something you would love so much,' Catherine smothered her giggles at the child's devotion to his new belonging, for she had been with James as he made an anguished decision about what to take home to his small son.

'We chose well then, James,' she smiled at him and they sat companionably on Daniel's bed and watched him play. 'What a gorgeous boy, just like his daddy. His mother must have been divine, he will break hearts, you mark my words,' and they hugged, James delighted by Catherine's reaction to his son.

Later, as they sat in James's study, going through the plans for Catherine's visit, she turned to him and said, 'You must be so happy, on your return, to find Daniel so loved and minded. Peg is an angel here on earth, and Aileen seems a fine girl. As for Carissa, her lovely name suits her lovely face.'

'Her mother had a very hard pregnancy with Carissa, Catherine. She was terribly ill throughout, and then her pains came early. She and her husband, Liam, who is now deceased, prayed to the Heart of Jesus for her survival.'

Catherine raised her shoulders in query and gestured for him to continue.

'Irish people believe in the Sacred Heart of Jesus, surrounded with its thorns and burning flames of love, and have a special devotion to the image. Anyway, the baby girl survived and indeed thrived. And so, in thanks, they called her *Croí Íosa*, Heart of Jesus, and in time that became Carissa.'

They all sat around the table, eating, drinking, and laughing at Daniel's conversation. Even Edward, who had returned from his afternoon's sport, smiled at the boy.

'And wait until you see Galway, Catherine, it is wonderful,' James was saying. 'Carissa, say a few words in Irish for our visitors. Please?'

Carissa hated being pushed forward under the gaze of all assembled there, but did as she was asked.

'Oh my dear, what a pretty language,' Catherine smiled at her.

'It is that,' replied James, 'but I would like Carissa to learn more English, and it would help Daniel in turn, I think.'

'Well then, I have a simple solution. The Bible!' said Catherine, looking triumphantly around the table at the guests.

'The Bible?' he replied, perplexed.

'Yes James, you do have one?'

'Well, no,' he said shamefacedly, shuffling in his seat.

Catherine laughed at him and took his hand, 'Well you must purchase one, I can recommend the King James version, which is written beautifully. Carissa can read aloud from it and you can supervise her lessons. Perfect!' She paused, 'Oh my dear Carissa, I didn't mean to offend you by not asking your opinion. I just thought it would be a good way to start to improve your English.'

Carissa took a deep breath, then blew out the feelings of annoyance that not being included in the discussion brought her. 'Thank you, Catherine. I think it is perfect,' she smiled.

On leaving that evening, as the shadows had deepened into night's gathering gloom, Charles leaned down from his horse to speak to Carissa. 'You will join us, I trust, at the picnic?'

She looked to James, he noted her flushed cheeks, and nodded yes.

'Well, then, that is settled, we will meet again in two days.' He gave her a dazzling grin before urging his horse onwards.

'Catherine, my love, I will see you then,' said James through the open window of the carriage, where she sat with Edward, who was delighted to have her all to himself.

He smiled at his beautiful cousin as the carriage took off, and started to speak as James Quinn was left behind to wave them goodbye.

They stood by the cascading water, holding hands as Daniel jumped up and down excitedly, pointing at the waterfall, small toy boat in his hands. His words were drowned out by the roar, but it was clear that he wanted to sail it.

James smiled at Catherine and pulled her gently away from the noise and splashing water which had wet the bottom of her gown. Rainbows formed as the spume hit the pool and wet mist rose.

'James, how magnificent! My heart is racing,' Catherine told him once they were a few paces away and could hear themselves again.

He squeezed her hand. 'It would seem that Daniel is very keen to sail his boat. Do you mind, dear?'

'Of course not! I shall act as sailor to his captain and we will have a grand time,' and she took the boy's hand and led him to where a grassy bank seemed dry under their hands and knees and the river rippled only slightly.

'Now Daniel,' she said, 'you tell me what to do, because I fear I am not very good at sailing fine vessels such as this.'

'It's a boat, silly lady,' and he fell about laughing at her foolishness.

Catherine looked back a while later to see that a blanket had been laid on the grass, and Peg and Carissa had laid out a picnic for them all to share.

'Daniel, let us go and have something to eat. It will give

us energy for more sailing later,' she said to the boy and he took the boat out of the water and shook it dry, droplets glinting silver in the sun.

'Here are our brave mariners, returned from their adventures at sea,' said James, as he looked up and saw them approaching. 'Well Daniel, were there any giant fish in the water?'

The child's eyes grew round as he recounted Catherine's tales of a great scaly fish living at the bottom of the river who loved picnics, so they must be wary and guard their food closely.

'Even here in Wicklow there are such fish?' James asked his son, and the little boy nodded fervently. 'You are very brave then, but should eat up so that it doesn't get your food!'

'My, it is hot for September,' said Catherine, raising her parasol above her head.

Daniel looked at her. 'Is there rain, Catherine?' he asked, confused as the sky above was bright blue and the sun shone, a fiery orb.

She smiled at him, 'No Daniel, dear heart, bless you, but ladies like me do not like to get too brown or freckly.'

'Enough questions for now, Daniel,' said Carissa. 'Let us go and have a wander around and see if there are any birds making their nests in the trees today.'

'I will clear up and shake out the blanket,' Peg said, and Catherine took James's arm as they headed off for a stroll among the lush greenery and ivy-wrapped trees.

'My father sends his best,' she said to him.

'He is well?'

'Yes, on a hunting trip in Wales,' she replied, and they fell into easy conversation about her life in London and people he had met while at her Cavendish home.

'Have you been to see Father's tailor yet?'

He plucked at his clothes and sniffed, 'Doesn't look like it, does it?'

She laughed at him and pushed him playfully.

'Daniel is very taken with you, Catherine,' James said, and stopped walking, turning to face her.

'And I am taken too, James. He is pure, beautiful, warm sunshine,' she smiled up at him and he gathered her in his arms and bent his head to kiss her.

Carissa glanced at the waterfall, and, a little to the left, saw them kiss. She smiled. She looked at the waterfall again, and a little to the right, hidden to view unless you looked very closely, she saw Charles and Edward clasping hands in a way that she had never seen men do before. Daniel tugged at her skirts and she looked down at her small charge, flustered.

James sat on Daniel's bed, the candlelight glimmering around the room, making the shadows of the nursery furniture and toys flicker and dance, large on the walls. He tucked his son in and told him of his visit to Dublin Castle with Catherine.

He had gone no more than a few sentences into his tale when he turned to his son. 'Honestly, Daniel, if you keep on asking me "why", it will be tomorrow morning by the time we are finished!' and he tickled the boy, who promised to be quiet for the rest of the story, thumb in his mouth, blanket in his hand as he looked up at his daddy, tracing the shadows on the wall with his other hand.

'So, then, Catherine sat on the throne like a queen. A throne is like a special seat, Daniel, for very important people, and this one was a gift to William III when he conquered King James at the battle of the River Boyne in

1690. A different James, Daniel. Not me, sadly, I am no king,' he smiled down at his son.

'Anyway, she looked like a beautiful queen and she was happy. And then we had a tour of the castle and you would have loved it, Daniel. I shall bring you one day.

'The guide, Sean, told us of the Viking invaders when Dublin was called Dyflinn after a black pool that they built their fortress around.' James paused and saw that the child was beginning to get sleepy.

'Well, then Sean showed us the old, old tower, and into the castle defences. And across the central square, down worn steps lit by a spluttering torch, until, at last, we stood at the very base of the powder tower in a great cavern.'

James had been painting pictures with his hands for the child, but saw that his eyes were closing, so gathered him closer and laid his son's head on his chest. Daniel sighed.

'After that, we went to the grand apartments and had music from the Vice-Regal state band, the Dublin city band, the Anacreontic Society, and the Irish Harp ensemble, with their jigs, reels, hornpipes and slow airs – Catherine loved that bit, Daniel. And then we met my friend Surgeon Stone.'

Daniel was fast asleep, his head heavy on James's chest. He eased his son off him and laid him back on the bed, tenderly, and kissed his forehead, tucking him in snug once more.

'And Daniel,' he spoke to the sleeping form below him, 'she made a pretence of forgetting her gloves, and I went back down into the dark bowels of the castle with her, and she had them with her all along, and she drew me close and we kissed.

'Her lips are so soft, Daniel. I can still feel them on mine.' He leaned over, blew out the candle, and tiptoed from the room.

Carissa sat stock-still in the adjoining room, candle long extinguished, the door to her room open to Daniel's, as always. James had not known she was there, relaxing on her bed, looking out the window at the starry, dreamy sky.

She slumped down onto her bed, tears flowing, wrapped her arms around herself against the cold loneliness, and turned her face into the pillow, wetting it with her heartache.

19

A powder for cleaning the teeth

Chop up a handful of mint and sage very small. Mix
these into a half ounce of the cream of tartar and a
quarter ounce of the powder of myrrh. Stir this up well
and keep it in a covered jar or a cup. You may rub it onto
your teeth once or twice a week.

Quinn Household Recipes and Remedies Book

Aileen sat on the bed in her sister's room and watched her,
a frown marring her pretty face. All she had heard since
she arrived earlier this evening was 'Catherine this' and
'Catherine that'. So different from the conversation they
had before her visit, when it seemed like Carissa would turn
away rather than say a kind word to the English woman. She
had seen Carissa observe Catherine closely, and her sister
had obviously taken some of her mannerisms as her own.

As Aileen watched, Carissa turned and twisted in front
of the mirror to get a better view of herself in the new
silken gown, her hair up and caught at the back with pearls,
a different curve to her cheek, lip and eyelash, thanks to
some of Catherine's beauty remedies. She was even using a
powder to clean her teeth. Aileen sighed.

'Catherine thinks I should come out for the Season,' she said to Aileen, patting her hair as if some of it had escaped its confines.

'Does our kind even do that?'

'What do you mean, "our kind", Aileen? I am a fine young woman, so Catherine says, and look the part, but I still need to improve my English,' she twirled a curl around her little finger. The language was difficult to master, as it was without a trace of the cadences and softness of her mother tongue. 'You should learn it too, Aileen, and then we will both be fine young women.'

'To please ourselves or the English woman? She seems to have made you her pet project and I miss the way my sister used to be.'

'What did you say?'

'Nothing, Carissa, nothing.'

Daniel sat on the floor, playing with the two-masted schooners his father had bought him for his birthday.

'And in the beginning, God created the heavens and the Earth,' Carissa intoned to her mirror, Bible in her hand, as she addressed an unseen audience, Daniel on the floor with his ships and Aileen on the bed.

'Every evening, would you believe it, we sit and discuss stories from the Bible. First he reads, and then I must follow. Aileen, it is hard, but my English has improved so much.' She sat on the bed beside her sister. 'When I say the words as if they were written to be pronounced in Irish, James becomes all agitated, with his face reddening as he tries to conceal his impatience. Peg and Daniel laugh, and then he becomes even more flustered. After that I suddenly remember how to say the words as he spoke them – it's such fun,' she laughed.

'So I can hear, sister, and I think you tease and flirt with him all of the time. What about Charles?'

'Not true, not true,' Carissa blushed, then said softly, 'and Charles. Aileen, he showed me such attention, but then at the picnic I saw him hold Edward's hands.' She turned to the Bible.

'Have you never seen men do that before, Carissa?'

'I don't know; it just seemed different somehow. But look,' she said, changing the subject, 'see, this is how we choose where to read from,' and she closed her eyes and then opened the book.

'So what does it say, or can you actually read in the absence of James's guiding hand?'

Carissa sent her a withering look and began to read. 'Now Sari, Abram's wife, bare him no children: and she had a handmaid, an Egyptian, whose name was Hagar.' She cleared her throat in an exaggerated manner and continued.

'And Sari said unto Abram, Behold now, the Lord hath restrained me from bearing: I pray thee go unto my maid; it may be that I may obtain children by her.' Carissa quickly closed her eyes and chose a new passage from the book.

James Quinn sat at his desk, writing up the cases from the day. He smiled as he reread the letter that he had received from William Smyley in response to his own. It seemed that the cat Abraham had been busy going forth and multiplying and now William and Eupham were knee deep in black and tabby kittens. Knowing his kind-hearted one-time hosts, he could imagine that the feline babies would stay, unless alternative homes could be found for them.

He stretched in his seat and smothered a yawn as the voice of a woman came to his ears. Leaving his desk, he opened the door and walked into the corridor.

The conversation was coming from Carissa's bedroom, but surely Aileen had bid them all farewell earlier in the day? James knew that Daniel was downstairs helping Peg to make their evening meal. So who was in there with her?

He walked to her door, and got ready to knock. But his hand fell to his side and he did not call out as he realised that Carissa was alone.

'Let him kiss me with the kisses of his mouth, for thy love is better than wine,' she said in her soft voice. 'Thy lips are like a thread of scarlet, and thy speech is comely, thy temples are like a piece of pomegranate within thy locks, thy two breasts are like two young roes that are twins, which feed among the lilies.'

James turned away, feeling he knew not what, as the beautiful verses of the Songs of Solomon echoed in his mind.

'I did good helping Peg, Daddy. I hope you eat it all up,' Daniel looked up solemnly at his father, who was seated beside him at the table.

Peg and Carissa smiled fondly at father and son from their places.

'It is delicious, Daniel. You have a great talent, thank you.'

'I will make it every day,' the child, mouth full of food, replied.

James looked around at his son and the women, and remarked, 'I have eaten my honeycomb with my honey; I have drunk my wine and my milk; eat, O friends, and drink, yea, drink abundantly, O beloved.'

Peg looked on quizzically, lost, as he continued.

The blood drained from Carissa's face as she realised that James was quoting from the same pages of the Bible she had just read quietly to herself in her bedroom – he must have overheard her. Oh, the shame. A deep blush rose from her chest and painted her pale complexion with crimson, burning heat.

'How fair and how pleasant art thou, O love,' said James, as he took more food from the serving bowl.

Carissa stood up quickly, unable to take any more, and then bolted from the room as her skirts caught on her chair and brought it to the floor with a clatter. Daniel looked on in amazement and James raised his eyebrow and shrugged his shoulders, all innocence. Peg stared at James and slowly shook her head.

'Carissa didn't like her food, Daddy?'

'Here present,' wrote Matthew Carter as the men assembled in the magnificent Library of Trinity College, 'on this day, the first of the month of October, 1741:

'Master Surgeon Laurence Stone, Physician Ryan, man-midwife practitioners Bartholomew Mosse, Fielding Ould, Thomas Southwell, Matthew Carter and James Quinn, Apothecary John Caldwell.

'For discussion: The plight of women with child in Dublin.'

'In recent times,' spoke Surgeon Stone, 'I have become gravely concerned about the plight of our mothers, especially those of the lower orders who deserve our charity. I have toiled for nigh on thirty years at surgery with a fair share of midwifery cases. I can find no room for complacency on the subject of mothers with child in this city.'

He observed that Carter could not keep pace. 'Matthew, you may simply enclose the document I submitted to all of you with the details I now lay before you. You are, after all, a man-midwife and not a scribe,' he smiled at the man seated before him, earnest in his task.

Matthew looked up and nodded, but continued to write.

'May I call to mind the gracious lady Mrs Mary Mercy, the Lord be good to her soul, who built an alms house, in St Peter's parish, for poor ladies. As many as twenty could be accommodated at a time, in four large, well-appointed rooms. To my great disappointment, the alms house was turned over to a different use some seven or so years ago.

'And now no beds may be availed of for childbirth in any Dublin hospital. I place this dire matter here before you in the true and certain hope that an answer may be found to these women's sufferings. I thank you for your forbearance and now would like you to debate the matter.'

As Surgeon Stone sat, Bartholomew Mosse stood to address the meeting. 'The misery of the poor women of the city of Dublin, at the time of their lying-in, would scarcely be conceived by anyone who had not been an eyewitness to their wretched circumstances,' he spoke fervently, with great sincerity.

'Their lodgings are generally in cold garrets, open to every wind, or in damp cellars, subject to floods from excessive rains.'

'What of it, Mosse?' Physician Ryan, who wished a hasty conclusion to the meeting and appeared even more tetchy than usual, barked out. 'The difficulties you describe should rightfully be resolved by the Irish Parliament under the direction of the Lord Lieutenant. We bear no responsibility whatsoever in this matter.'

Matthew dropped his quill to the table, ink spots blossoming over his papers. A quarrel was about to erupt, and Lord, he hated arguments. He rubbed his face, leaving ink there where his hand had touched it.

'Not so, I say. We must fight on behalf of the women,' Mosse was upset with the physician's manner. 'They themselves are destitute of attention, medicines, and often of proper food, so hundreds perish with their little infants, and the community is at once robbed of mother and child. I consider that it is our sacred duty to amend the circumstances placed before you.'

'Such passion, Mosse,' Physician Ryan leaned back in his chair and tapped his cane noisily on the wooden floor. 'Perhaps the combustion you exhibit is better suited to the hustings at a political rally. University graduates such as we,' he paused as if forgetful. 'Oh of course, *mea culpa*, I do beg your pardon, dear boy.' Ryan was fully aware that only he of those present was a university graduate, as the others had served apprenticeships.

He went on, 'We of higher learning must remain calm in the face of whatever adversity befalls us. I must tell you, frankly, that I consider the practice of midwifery by male practitioners as a disreputable field of endeavour that should lie entirely in the domain of midwives – with occasional assistance from surgeons and apothecaries.'

Fielding Ould jumped to his feet and protested, 'But the College of Physicians was entrusted with the examining and licensing of midwives in its Founding Charter. Can you confirm that during those fifty years only four persons, including some here present, were so examined? I say, sir, that you abrogate on your responsibilities!'

'And you, sir,' spat back Ryan, 'may have a licence in midwifery but dare I say that you did not graduate as a physician. The College of Physicians will soon refuse to consult with any or all persons who are not graduates of our college, and that includes most here present. You practise a purely mechanical, laborious art that is derogatory to the dignity of academic medicine.'

James was on his feet, voice shaking with anger as he spoke, 'That will be an absurd injustice to commit against man-midwives and will only further harm the women of Dublin.'

'Perhaps you should consider a return to Paris, young man, the city you extol for its virtues in midwifery. From there you may all write to the Lord Lieutenant, as indeed I may do, and at some distant time he may see fit to resolve your anguish.' Ryan rose to his feet. 'Meanwhile, gentlemen, *adieu*, for there is work to be done.' And with a curt bow he turned and strode down the length of the shelves, full to the brim with academic texts, and out of the library door.

As the men watched his retreating back, Surgeon Stone raised his hands, saying, 'Be at ease and remember his words – this is a time for calm in the face of adversity. We have business to conclude here today.'

And so they settled back into the meeting, Matthew once again happily taking notes as Bartholomew Mosse outlined his great plans to develop a hospital for women in childbirth; a hospital that would be administered and staffed by midwives and man-midwives for the betterment of the women, children and families of Dublin.

'Thank you so much, I loved my birthday meal,' said James, patting his stomach contentedly, 'and all my favourites too, how did you know?' He looked at Peg, Carissa, and Daniel, who were smiling happily at him. 'Really Peg, thank you, from the bottom of my heart.'

'Well now James, I must tell you, it was all Carissa's doing, her hard work.'

James looked at Carissa in astonishment, 'I had no idea you were such a fine cook. Peg will have to let you prepare our meals more often. Thank you then, Carissa.' He stood and pushed back his chair, 'But birthday or no, I still have case notes to write, so I will take my leave and see you all later.'

Carissa breathed out in relief as he left the room. Peg laughed and turned to Daniel, saying, 'You were a precious boy, not to give away our little secret.'

The boy smiled at her, and put his finger to his lip, giggling impishly.

'But Carissa, I am not so sure that you should be doing all the cooking from now on!'

Earlier that day, Carissa lay on her bed rereading the letter from James's mother in reply to her own asking what her son's favourite dishes were, as she wished to cook him a birthday meal. The two women had become very close over the years.

'My dear,' she read, 'what a very lovely idea, and how sweet of you to think of it. James has a fondness for many foods, now that I think of it, but he has some special favourites. I shall enclose some recipes with my letter for you.'

And she had. A fish soup, thick and chunky, with tasty morsels of pollack and salted herring competing for flavour with delicious portions of scallop. 'To be served with slices of brown bread spread with salty butter to mop up the succulent sauce,' Mother Quinn had written in her neat hand.

'To be followed by mutton stew, James's favourite dish. The stew should be cooked from early morning and simmered for hours over a low heat. It will remind him of his childhood when his father came home late, tired and hungry. James would sit on his knee and relish small spoonfuls of the stew and savour every mouthful of his special treat.

'The meat should be so tender that he could suck every last piece off the bone. The potatoes, carrots and onions to be so soft that they fall into the thick rich gravy and enhance it even more.

'With, perhaps, an extra serving of boiled potatoes, their jackets split open to reveal their floury hearts, to be smothered in butter.

'The dessert, I leave to you, as my son has such a sweet tooth that just about anything will satisfy.'

Carissa folded the letter neatly and decided to make apple pie with fresh cream from the dairy just around the corner from their home, St Patrick's Close. Or mouth-watering Irish plum cake. And to follow, the final dish of Dutch cheese, served with buttermilk or green tea.

'Carissa, dear, are you ready? You need to start cooking if it is all to be ready in time,' Peg's disembodied voice climbed the stairs to where she lay.

She left her room and went to the kitchen. Once inside the room, she boldly approached the chopping board.

'Can you kindly remind me which way I carve the meat into nice proper pieces, Peg,' she asked imploringly.

Peg looked at her, noting her worried face and hands that twisted the fabric of her skirt between them. She laughed, 'Why not start with chopping the vegetables, dear, and I will cook the fish and the meat. But you will have to learn more on cookery if you are to one day be married.' Carissa blushed with embarrassment but said that if Peg would cook for her, she would, in return, take care of Peg's children. Then she stopped, as it seemed such an unlikely possibility because Peg was a confirmed, happy spinster.

She looked at Peg and they both laughed as Daniel looked on, bemused, and Carissa bent down to him saying, 'Not even a whisper to your daddy about Peg helping me out.' She straightened up. 'But I will learn, Peg, because I want to be able to cook for my husband, when the proper time comes.'

20

To calm a sharp fever
Take a cup of fine ale and add to it a good spoonful of
treacle, a powdered nutmeg, a sprinkling each of salt and
Jamaica pepper. Mix these together and take three times
every day until the fever does not return.

Quinn Household Recipes and Remedies Book

The early morning light bewitched her, adding lustre to her
already bountiful, shining hair, turning her dark eyes into
fathomless pools, sowing extra roses in her cheeks.

James looked at Catherine as she surveyed the assembled
company that sat in his drawing room before they left to
attend Mr Handel's *Messiah*. She was radiant today.

They were all in their finery, an air of excitement
breathed in and out from every person, save Aileen who
was staying behind to mind Daniel, but that in itself was
treat enough for her; she was just sorry not to be as finely
dressed as everyone else in the room.

Peg sat and plucked at the delicate lace on her chest,
Carissa was beautiful in her new gown, Catherine's sister
Alice beamed and twinkled, her fingers restless, eager to be
off. Edward sat stiffly, glowering now and again in James's

direction. And Catherine, as always, took centre stage and sparkled in body and person.

'For pity's sake, let James read to us of our upcoming adventure!' she said, and clapped her hands for silence.

He shook out the Saturday edition of the *Dublin News Letter* and read, 'Yesterday morning, at the Musick Hall, there was a public rehearsal of *Messiah*, Mr Handel's new sacred oratorio, which, in the opinion of the best judges, far surpasses anything of that nature which has been performed in this or any other Kingdom.' He peered over the top of the paper, and seeing their interest continued.

'The elegant entertainment was conducted in the most regular manner, and to the entire satisfaction of the most crowded and polite assembly. To the benefit of three very important public charities, there will be a grand performance of this oratorio on Tuesday next, 13 April 1742, in the forenoon.'

'Here, let me read for you from *Faulkner's Dublin Journal*,' said Catherine excitedly, '"The *Messiah* was rehearsed to a most grand, polite and crowded audience." And what will they write about us fair beauties tomorrow morning, I wonder?' She shushed the laughs that followed with, '"It is requested as a favour that ladies who honour this performance with their presence attend without hoop skirts, as it will greatly increase the charity by making room for more company." Hmm, I feel inadequately clothed without my hoop frames,' she said and Carissa blushed at her forthright speech.

James began to read again, 'The gentlemen are desired to come without their swords, to increase audience accommodation yet further, I would say. For all six hundred tickets are sold and I am sure that more will make their way in to see such a grand event.'

'Oh, what excitement!' Catherine was on her feet, 'We must away or be late! The tickets, James, I believe they are in your care?'

James fanned the tickets out in front of him and they walked to the waiting carriages.

'*Tá tú go háilinn*, Carissa. You look beautiful,' Aileen whispered to her sister, clasping her hand. Carissa threw her sister a grateful look and departed in a swish of silken skirts.

'Thomas Neal's Musick Hall, Fishamble Street, sir?' James nodded assent to their driver and they moved off.

'I love that you complimented all of us on our attractiveness, but I did not hear any murmur from you about Carissa,' Catherine admonished James light-heartedly, 'I think you look quite beautiful today my dear,' she smiled at her.

'Why do we worry about clothes? See how the lilies of the field grow in such splendour. Yet the beauty of the lily of Galway far exceeds my words of description,' said James, and Carissa felt the all-too-familiar blush start to rise again. 'There is but one and only Carissa, and some day, a young man will steal her heart.'

'James you tease too much; forgive him, dearest Carissa. I do hope our seating will be commodious and situated well,' she said, opening her fan and changing the conversation with a wave of cool air to her face.

The music hall was formed in the shape of an ellipse, and divided into the pit, the boxes and the lattices. Its seats were covered in lush scarlet and fringed, while stuffed handrails gave them the form of luxury couches. The ceiling was exquisitely painted, a drop curtain sat over the stage, drawn with an azure sky in a cloudscape from which emerged Apollo's lyre, and the pilasters were cased with mirrors and nearby figures were painted on white ground relieved with gold. All around, the theatre was festooned with golden cords and tassels.

Catherine leaned over and spoke in James's ear, 'What a wonder; this concert hall befits the Second City of the Empire, don't you think? Did you know that Laurence Whyte has extolled its virtues in a charming poem? "As Amphion built of old the Theban wall, So Neal has built a sumptuous Musick Hall".'

'Perhaps if Mr Whyte wrote on childbirth I may be better read,' James replied into her ear, and was rewarded with a smart slap on the wrist.

The choirs of boys and men filed slowly on stage, followed by the principal singers, and loud, animated chatter filled the auditorium. Thomas Neal took to the stage and a hush fell over the audience.

'Dear patrons of the arts,' he said, arms thrown wide, expansive, effusive in his greeting, 'welcome to our new Musick Hall, where we wait impatiently in anticipation of Mr Handel's sacred grand oratorio, *Messiah*, the anointed one.

'Soon we shall hear the sublime, the grand, the tender, and the most elevated words adapted from scripture by Mr Charles Jennens and set to music by Mr Handel, music to transport and charm the ravished heart. The four hundred pounds raised by your donations was generously donated by Mr Handel to be equally shared by the Society for Relieving Prisoners, the Charitable Infirmary, and Mercer's Hospital.

'The choirs of St Patrick's and Christchurch Cathedrals, Matthew Dubourg who will lead the orchestra, our soprano Signora Christina Maria Avoglio and contralto Susannah Arne Cibber, will all perform their parts to admiration, acting on the same principle of pious charity, being satisfied only by the applause of you, the public.

'At the conclusion of the rehearsal on Friday last, Mr Handel remarked to me, "I would be sorry if I only entertained them; I wished to make them better." Now pray silence, ponder those words and show your attention for Mr Handel.'

Ringing, sustained applause followed for the large man who walked on stage and sat at the harpsichord.

'His father was a surgeon,' Catherine said, and James wondered idly if Daniel might one day compose wondrous music.

As the sacred words of the Birth, the Passion and the Aftermath set to such soaring music as to reach the heavens swept over them, Catherine wept tears of joy, while Carissa sobbed in sorrow as she remembered her father's illness and death. James held their hands in turn, all the while transfixed by the power and the glory of the words and music.

The audience was so entirely overcome by their emotions that when the music eventually died, their drained bodies could hardly rise – but stamp and holler and clap they did, ovation on ovation.

Catherine and James became separated in the crush of rushing bodies as the hall emptied, disgorging its occupants into its entrance and to the street outside. The noise was deafening.

Suddenly James was pushed forward by the surging tide of musical evacuees, and thrust against soft feminine buttocks. He slid his left arm around their owner's waist in order to steady both himself and her. Carissa turned to face him, moving her body against his. Another push of people saw them trapped against the theatre wall, limb to limb, pressed, pushed so firmly together as to almost melt into each other and become one.

James loosened his right arm to steady them all the more by placing it on the wall. His hand moved along her thigh, then up over her waist, passing slowly, dangerously close to her bosom. As his hand reached the wall above him, James's chin touched her hair and the fragrance of her perfume wafted through his consciousness. When he bent to apologise for the crush, his lips were tickled by the hair that brushed against his mouth.

She looked up at him, her lips framing the gilded cage of her own lovely mouth, her pink tongue ready to articulate, her cheeks flushed, her chest aglow with red blotches, a furious pulsation in her neck.

The crowd surged once more, and their embrace continued, but more languorous now, Carissa left with the indelible imprint of his body on hers.

Then all changed once more and their bodies were dragged apart.

Catherine moved away from the sight of James and Carissa as quickly as she could, and put her hand to her forehead as she walked, feeling how damp it was. She had been watching for some time. Today it had all became crystal clear, and the inner voice that had nagged and niggled at her during her visit would be silenced no more. She needed to sit down. She held her stomach. The nausea rose again. She wanted some fresh air and to be away from the press of bodies. She was horribly dizzy and looked around for a gap in the throng in which to make her escape. She thought she might be sick there and then, and her mouth filled with bilious liquid.

Her salvation appeared in the guise of Edward, who noted her pale face with a stab of worry. He pulled her into his arms and helped her outside, pushing anyone who stood in their path away in a none-too-gentlemanly manner.

'Catherine, are you quite well?' he asked once they were outside, and seeing his worried face she dissolved into tears. He held her gently and she allowed herself to be shushed by his calm embrace.

'Edward, I want to go home,' she spoke into his chest, words small and muffled.

'To my father's estate?'

'No,' she pushed herself out of his embrace and looked him in the eye. She brushed her tears away almost impatiently. 'Back to London. Edward, will you come with me?'

'I would be delighted, Catherine,' he replied, and as he held her close again he couldn't help the smile that formed his lips into a curve, or the sense of satisfied delight that swelled within him.

'Dada, can you hear me up in Heaven? Oh please, Dada, you must help me!' Carissa laid her head on Daniel's bed, knees numb from kneeling on the floor by his side, damp sheet in one hand while the other held a cold cloth to the boy's forehead. She could hear his breath wheezing in and out, and his obvious painful discomfort brought forth a fresh flurry of tears. She sobbed.

'Please Dada, bring James back so he might see how ill Daniel is. His poor little body is racked with it Dada, look!'

All that dreadful, bleak day, Daniel was overcome with chills and shivering, heat and cold coming in quick succession. She felt so helpless; her soft words and cuddles did nothing for the boy.

Now he lay in a fitful sleep with her at his side. She comforted him as best she could, although he did not notice, crooning gently, soaking his hot skin with cooled water and not a few tears, holding him when he shivered, removing the bedclothes when he burned in the throes of a violent fever, tossing and turning, moaning in distress, crying out.

'Dada!' she cried. 'Please tell Marguerite her son is so terribly sick. Please. She must – you must – be able to do something, please! I am so frightened, I love him so much, don't let him be taken away.'

That night, Carissa felt the terrors take her. She was by herself, James called out on a case and Peg in bed, deeply asleep having minded Daniel the night before. She did not yet know enough of herbal medicine to help, though Mairin had started to teach her before she came to Dublin, and Carissa made a vow that if Daniel recovered she would learn more so that she would never feel so helpless again.

She trembled, the shadows in the once homely nursery becoming menacing, snarling beasts, trying to get Daniel and steal him from her in their jagged, slavering maws.

In the early morning, Daniel closed his swollen eyes tightly, as the weak sunlight caused him such pain. He cried pitifully with sickness and drank great, thirsty gulps of cold water. Then began the coughing, dry at first, and later with nose streaming; he was sneezing and snuffling and miserable.

She heard the front door open and shouted out for help. James ran upstairs to the nursery and, eyes heavy with tiredness from his night's work, saw his son and heard her story. Carissa could have wept again for the sorrow and worry she saw in James's face, but then the learning in him took over and he rushed out of the room, calling over his shoulder that he would return with Physician O'Rourke.

'Thank you, Dada, thank you, Marguerite,' Carissa whispered, and took the suffering child's hands in hers, her thumb moving in slow circles across his hot flesh as he slipped into an uneasy sleep once more.

Physician O'Rourke was charming and kind, but Carissa still kept a watchful eye on Daniel as he was examined, wincing as the child squirmed and cried out in pain when his stomach was pressed.

'There now, little fellow,' said O'Rourke, 'we shall soon have you up and about, and you were very brave when I had to touch your body with my cold hands. My other patients complain, but not you, brave boy.' He pulled the bedclothes up to Daniel's chin and patted his hand. 'James, if we could step outside and have a word.'

James nodded and the men went downstairs to his study as Carissa resumed her place by Daniel's side.

'My diagnosis is that Daniel has been struck down with roseola, an eruptive catarrhal fever, generally epidemic, and currently rife in the vicinity. Soon an eruption will be at hand, rendering his face variously spotted, and then descending to the chest, belly and thighs in great coalesced red and brown blotches. We see much of this illness, James, so much that I can write you the problems as they will manifest on a day-by-day calendar.

'The roseola is not dangerous to life, except from an insalubrious constitution in some, the very young, and the very old. Those who are in peril must survive through the ninth day - yet I perceive Daniel as a strong child and my prognosis is good. Be aware that others in this household may fall victim to the illness too.'

'My heartfelt thanks to you, Patrick. We were very worried for him,' said James, and he shook the physician's hand warmly. 'But what must we do about the fever that accompanies this roseola measles? What about Peruvian Bark, will it help?'

The physician stroked his chin thoughtfully before replying. 'There is a little doubt, but the bark is most useful for quartan fevers, so Daniel may well benefit from the medication. And tincture solution in alcohol of the Peruvian Bark has long been held in esteem.'

'But if the stomach is a little tender, as Daniel's is, what then?' enquired James.

'If the stomach is tender, a decoction prepared in water may be used. Here, I will write a fit remedy for you.'

Once he had seen O'Rourke out, James returned to the nursery to tell Carissa. She had fallen asleep clutching Daniel's hand. He prised their hands apart as gently as he could and carried her to her own bed, telling Peg all that had happened as she held her hand to her mouth and then to her heart before she rushed upstairs from the kitchen to sit with Daniel.

The apothecary worked his magic like an alchemist of old, sweating in the heat of his compounding room. When the red transparent liquor was poured off, a change of colour to yellow came upon the liquid.

Boiling of the bark in fresh water was repeated until the liquor became transparent when it cooled off. The decoctions were strained and mixed together over a gentle fire to the point of evaporation. From the remaining extract, medicine was prepared in the form of a powder, which was then spooned into syrup mixed with water.

Daniel's fever responded to the medicine but he was miserable for days. Carissa initially refused to leave his side, and only then under strict instruction from James and Peg to get some sleep.

Then, one morning shortly afterwards, Carissa was unable to rise from her bed, and she slipped into a feverish state, raving with the heat mania when the ague bit deeply into her under-slept body. Her forehead was sweaty and her hair stuck to her face. Large dark-brown rings appeared under her eyes.

James sat with her then, spooning the same medicine that had helped Daniel into her mouth, past her cracked, dry lips, but it seemed to have little effect. He held Carissa's hand while reading his *Pharmacopoeia* to see what further medications could ease her.

As the ninth day approached, Carissa slipped deeper into her illness, and Patrick O'Rourke was called to the house once more. He placed his ear on her burning skin. 'It is in her chest now, James,' he said, his face betraying how worried he was for her.

That night they sat in vigil around Carissa's bedside by the light of a lone candle. James looked at her, ravaged by illness, and then at Peg and Daniel, his little face tense with fear. 'Please take Daniel to his bed and stay with him, Peg,' he said, and with a last glance at Carissa, Peg took the child's hand and led him out of the room.

James sank to his knees, put his elbows on her bed and prayed. 'Please Marguerite, help her. Help her,' he whispered.

A few days later, James smiled at Carissa, saying, 'It is a pectoral decoction for your chest with syrup of violets and maidenhair. You must take it four times a day.'

She wrinkled her nose and wanted to spit out the medicine that tasted so foul. He laughed at her, relieved that she was going to be well again, even though it might take some time yet.

'What is so amusing?' she glared up at him defiantly, voice cracked from her long illness.

'We are just glad to have you back with us. I am glad. You really worried us, Carissa.' He took her hand. 'Get better soon.'

She sat in a chair by the bed, weak and trembling in a shawl as Peg changed her sweat-soaked linen.

'I remember so little, Peg. I thought I was in Galway,' she whispered, as it still hurt to speak.

'You raved so much when the high fever was upon you,' said Peg, 'we were very worried for you.' She helped Carissa back into bed as gently as she could, tucking the bedclothes around her as she would with Daniel.

'Did I say anything terrible or tell my secrets?' Carissa was sick once more at the thought that she might have revealed her true feelings towards James, and she blushed.

'It would be easier to remember what you did not say,' replied Peg, noticing the blush that stained Carissa's pale cheeks.

'Oh no, tell me, tell me,' Carissa insisted, hand flying up to cover her mouth lest any more secrets find their way out.

'Hush, dear, and sleep,' Peg stroked Carissa's hair. 'Sleep and get better and return to us soon.' And she started to leave the room.

'Peg?'

'Yes, my dear?' and she turned at the doorway to look at Carissa.

'Nothing. Thank you for making me a fresh bed.'

Peg nodded her head and left the room.

When Carissa next woke, Daniel was standing by her bed, hands full of unkempt blooms he'd picked by himself. She struggled to sit up and kissed him on the forehead, 'I have missed you, my darling,' she said and he smiled at her.

Carissa lay back down again and fell asleep as Daniel gently stroked her hair.

'Did I do it right? Daddy did it like this.'

'Good boy, Daniel, good boy,' replied Peg.

21

To stew the neck of veal
Cut the neck into steaks and beat them flat. Season them with ground thyme, nutmeg, salt and pepper and fry them in your pan with cream. Then add into the mix some butter and broth and let them stew gently and stir them.

Quinn Household Recipes and Remedies Book

'Another letter. My word,' Peg arched her eyebrows, 'there must be something in the air. From Catherine, I'll wager,' and she tapped the note on her hand. 'As you are going to your room, Carissa, would you kindly deliver this epistle of love to James's study?'

Carissa knocked at the door but then remembered that James had departed in a hurry a short time ago. She entered the room and walked to the tall window that looked out on St Patrick's Close. It was a beautiful day, and the sun shone brightly. She felt happy.

She looked around the study, which was meticulously neat. Her gaze lighted on keepsakes from Paris, London and Galway, and she touched each one, straightening them afterwards, humming.

The portrait of Marguerite that had travelled with James to Paris sat on one side of the old wooden writing desk. His case studies were stacked in an orderly pile, while letters from Catherine peeked out from their pigeonhole. The quills, inkwells and sand cellar stood to attention on the other side of the desk. In the centre of it lay a single page of paper which had been written on but was unfinished.

Carissa was aware of the waft of perfume from the letter she held in her hand, and her thoughts turned to Catherine. She lived such a fancy life, but was so sweet and kind, especially to little Daniel. And though she was kind to Carissa too, she held James in the palm of her be-ringed hand.

She sighed and placed the letter on the desk beside the sheet. Her eyes fell on the paper, and she couldn't help herself. She read: 'My love. When I close my eyes I see your sweet face, and long for your gentle touch.'

Her eyes filled with tears and she could read no more. She was heartbroken. She dropped the sheet and ran out of the room, slamming the door behind her, the familiar corridor a soft, indistinct blur as the birds sang outside.

The needle and thread went through the fabric with a satisfying speed. Sewing quieted Carissa's mind, and it was still in the house, with both Peg and Daniel asleep upstairs. James was out at a call, and she sat in the cosy kitchen with her linen and thoughts, needle going in and out, in and out.

She started as the door opened and James came in. She looked up from her work and saw how tired he looked, but made no move to get up. He smiled at her, and she bent her head to her task once more.

He made his way over to the fireplace and heaped food from a pot kept warm there onto a plate. She heard him sit at the table and eat. She gathered her things and made to leave.

'Is all well with you, Carissa? You are very quiet,' he said.

She mumbled her reply, something about going to bed.

He did not hear her. 'Maybe the hour is too late for my lily of Galway to be up and about?' he asked playfully.

Still she did not respond and stood by the table, staring at the floor. 'Carissa?' he put his hand on her arm and she shrank back until she was against the wall.

He stood and went to her, hand outstretched to touch her face, and she pushed it away. 'Carissa, what bothers you? Have I upset you?'

She began to sob, and James put his arm around her shoulder, speaking softly to her, asking her what was wrong, comforting her. Carissa began to hit him, small ineffective blows glancing off his chest. She pulled at his coat, hands lashing out like a small endangered animal protecting her territory.

James caught her arms and pulled her close to him, 'Stop Carissa, stop!'

Then they were struggling, and as James tripped they slid to the ground. He held her tight still and she lay there, mantua and nightdress gathered around her knees, the soft, pale flesh of her legs on show.

He looked down at them and she fell limp and silent. He slowly loosened his hold on her, and he looked into her teary eyes, drops clinging to her lashes. He bent his head to kiss her and was disturbed by a soft cough from the door.

Peg stood there, her face crimson with embarrassment. And as James attempted an explanation about a friendly argument, Carissa darted away and they heard her run upstairs.

He followed her, and her door met his face as she slammed it shut. He knocked softly, beseeching, 'Carissa. Carissa, please, we must talk.' He heard her sobs.

'Go to your study. A letter waits there for you. Go and read how much she loves you!' she shouted and cried again, loudly, not caring that he heard her.

He turned from her door, shoulders slumped, and made his way to his study, footfalls heavy on the stair treads.

James sat in his chair, dejected, the letter unopened on his desk. He sighed; he would never understand women as long as he lived.

Mentor and pupil sat facing each other in generously padded armchairs, replete after a fine dinner attended by both men and Stone's three daughters, Emily, Edith and Eleanor. The surgeon joked that his dearly departed wife had loved the letter of the alphabet so much that she bestowed it lovingly upon the smaller, younger versions of herself.

James had never met Elizabeth Stone, but if her daughters were anything to go by she must have been a real beauty, and all three had inherited her dark hair and eyes, so their father told him proudly.

He was seated beside the eldest daughter, Emily, and when he complimented her on her appearance she blushed, making her even more pretty and appealing in that moment. He smiled before turning his attention back to the plate of veal in front of him.

'Well James, it appears quite clear to me,' said Laurence Stone, steepling his fingers, staring at them. 'In Paris, you discovered that your career can be hazardous; being blamed for poor outcomes at childbirth. In London, the man-midwife is ridiculed and challenged by midwives, and here … well, here your colleagues will pillory you and decry your true worth, and they may appear to obstruct what you would care to achieve on behalf of women, children and their families.'

'And what is so clear to you?' James asked quietly.

'I look to the future and see you work until you drop from tiredness. Your diligence will be rewarded with some unexpected kindnesses. You will be a reformer on behalf of your patients. You will gain the esteem of some colleagues and husbands, and the wrath of others. Amongst all of that, you will be the best man-midwife you can be.'

At the sight of his pupil's downcast face he smiled to himself, saying, 'Listen to yourself, James. You heart will know what to do.' He pulled out his pipe and lit it, and when it was obvious that no comment was forthcoming, he went on. 'My very good friend, a Jesuit, God be good to his soul, reminded me on one occasion that the ablest, kindest reformer of all times was crucified on a cross at Calvary. But now He sits at the right hand of God. You will know what is right; just make me proud when I look down at you through the pearly gates.'

'I pray you will not go there for many years, as I value your wise counsel,' James smiled at Stone, 'and thank you as always for helping me to clear my head and sort my thoughts.'

The surgeon smiled at James and nodded his head before turning to watch the smoke twisting its way up to the ceiling. 'I have no intention of going anywhere just yet, James. Besides, there is much for me yet to do and I have my three girls to look out for.'

'Gone? Carissa is gone? What do you mean, Peg?'

'Early this morning. She left this morning,' Peg's face was blotchy from the tears that she had shed, and she wrung her hands in distress.

'When will she return? What about Daniel? What about all of us?' James sat down heavily, gut churning. 'Why Peg, why did she leave us?'

'Affairs of the heart, romance. James—' Peg was interrupted by sharp knocking at the front door and when she went to answer it found a worried, breathless man standing there.

'My master needs Dr Quinn. Come quickly, come quickly,' he pleaded.

James sat back in the opulent carriage while the driver, the man who had just called to his door, drove hard towards their destination. They wheeled rapidly towards the open, ornate gates of a large townhouse and James sat forward in anticipation, hands dangling between his knees.

Physician Ryan sat downcast on the stairs outside the bedroom, the birth chamber of such horrors, and looked down at the doorway through which the dejected surgeon O'Neill had taken his leave a short time ago.

The forceps with which he had tried to effect the delivery had slipped off, and the woman's perineum, the soft, pliable muscle tissue that lay between the birth channel and the anus, lay torn and bleeding.

O'Neill advised that a man-midwife should be summoned with due haste, apologised that he could do no more and left the scene. The physician sent a prayer heavenward, pleading with God not to take his new love as he had taken his wife.

James was surprised when the careening carriage raced past his expected destination and sped off towards the tradespersons' area of Dublin, the Liberties, bouncing over the uneven cobblestones. His midwifery bag fell to the floor of the carriage, spilling its contents, and he was forced to bend and scoop his belongings back into the open mouth of the bag.

The physician found easing himself off the step the most difficult thing he had ever done, the weight of his worry bearing down on him, yet he entered the room where she lay, the centre of his world, sweating, face the colour of candle wax, bleeding.

The midwives had covered the young woman, hiding most of the bloody mess. He sat with her, and holding her hand, his past came crashing in on him in anguished waves. A wife carried away to an early death from consumption, children grown into adults, and a large townhouse shared by only himself and his memories. And so his work became his God, until one day this adorable woman came into his life. Less than half his age and she loved him, this hard, unforgiving man that he was.

But she would not grace his home; she felt her social standing would not allow it. And now he was about to lose her; every fibre of his being ached with love for her. Tears brimmed in his eyes.

James was jolted back in his seat as the driver's foot jammed hard on the brake pedal and shouts of 'Whoa! Whoa!' brought the carriage to rest outside the humble home. He jumped from the carriage and reached back in to retrieve his instrument case.

The sound of the carriage arriving drew the midwife to the window. She ran down the stairs, her shouts of, 'He's here, thank the good Lord,' following her descent, and she opened the front door for James. 'Upstairs, quickly, just follow me.'

James took the scene in at a glance – the father by the window, too scared and anxious to look back into the room, the worried midwives, the pale, sweating woman on the bed, hair stuck to the pillow. He drew back the bedclothes to reveal the bloody mess.

The man came to his side, taking James's hand roughly, holding it tight as he looked into his eyes. 'You must save her; she is my world, my life!'

James's eyes widened in recognition, but he slipped off his jacket, rolled up his sleeves, and got to work, casting concerned glances at the woman, offering what words of comfort he could as Ryan paced.

Once home later that evening, James opened the door of Daniel's bedroom to kiss his sleeping son.

The bed had not been slept in, and Daniel was nowhere to be seen. Worry clutched his heart and he rushed around, looking for the boy.

His heart slowed as he went into Carissa's room and saw Daniel curled up asleep there, thumb in his mouth as was his wont. He lay down beside his son, listening to his regular breathing, and allowed his mind to wander.

The anxiety, the sweat; so much blood today. The tiny baby that was born was slow to cry and would live an uncertain future. The young mother, torn, bloody, bruised would take months to recover. And the father.

Profuse in his thanks, Physician Ryan had embraced James as the tears of joy coursed down his cheeks, before he turned to the woman in the bed, lying there, pale and trembling. 'Oh well done, my darling, well done!' he had said and been so tender that James had to turn away. Turn away from the hateful thoughts of the man who loathed man-midwives, had been so quick to leave Marguerite to her fate, the man who had so recently been insufferable, uncaring and puffed up with his own self-importance at the meeting in Trinity College, and see him in a new light.

Early the next morning, Peg passed by Carissa's door on her way downstairs to wake the house. Glancing in, she saw father and son asleep on the bed, James holding Daniel.

'We must speak, James, about Carissa,' she said, over the remains of their breakfast.

'No, please, I will not allow it,' he said angrily, and pushed back his chair to leave.

Her hand on his arm stilled him, and she looked up at him and said, '*Éist a ghrá*, listen my love, for I know you better than most. Sit yourself down and just listen.' And when she was done, he pulled the crumpled letter from his pocket and passed it to Peg.

22

To comfort the heart
Make a water with the flowers of lily of the valley. Put the flowers in a glass jar of fine wine and stop the top. Leave this aside in a cool, dark place for four weeks and pour what mixture remains into a small phial. Take a drop on the tongue when you are in need.

Quinn Household Recipes and Remedies Book

London, 12 May 1742

My Dearest, Darling James,
Let me tell you a story.

Once upon a time there was a man, and his name was James. Now, he was a kind man, a handsome man, and he spent his days caring for women and their infants.

His life was not perfect; indeed, he had known great heartache. But his darkest times were past, and he had a beautiful young son and loving family.

Into his life came an English woman, and her name was Catherine. The two had a wonderful time, and indeed they loved each other. One day, Catherine crossed the great, stormy Irish Sea to meet her love and his young son, and to have many adventures together.

And they did.

However, James had a young girl who lived in his house and minded his son. Her name was Carissa. And Catherine saw how Carissa loved James. One day, they all went to see a wonderful musical event and Catherine was separated from James.

When she next saw him, he was in an embrace with one that was not her.

Now, Catherine's heart did not blacken with jealousy, for she knew that Carissa was kind and good, and rather a great sadness took her as she realised that her own story was not to have its happy ending after all.

And she shed many a tear.

But once in the comfort of her home in London she started to feel a little better, and to remember their time with great fondness. She knew that she would always carry the memories close to her heart and take them out to look at them now and again. Then she would smile.

So James, my darling James, as you read my letter know that I love you, and because of my love for you I must say, simply, go to her. People will say you could have made a better match, given that she is in your employ, but then people will always say things.

A part of my heart will always be yours, and I know that you and I will remain friends for all time.

My father had suspicious moisture around the eyes when I told him of this letter and he called you a rascal, his own dear word, seldom used, telling just how fond his thoughts are for you, and he wishes you well.

He has no need, however, to return to his old ways and threaten to sell me off to the highest bidder – jokingly and with love and my interests at heart, for sure – for Edward Burlington and I are to be married soon. A good match in his eyes, it pleases my father no end.

My father always called me his Princess, and in fact I am to be the Countess of Drumaline, as Edward's father passed away quite *suddenly and he will inherit all the land and fine manor house that goes with the title of Earl.*

Maybe you will find the time to visit us one day, after all we will not be so far from Dublin, and I would very much look forward to such an eventuality.

Always with deepest love and affection, my forever friend, and a kiss for your darling little mariner.

Catherine.

GALWAY, 1742

James Quinn sat up in the saddle and stretched, not noticing the rain that dribbled down from the brim of his hat into the space left between his collar and his neck.

He ached all over.

He leant down and murmured into Daniel's soft neck, 'We're nearly there, son, only a couple of miles left,' but the boy was asleep.

It had been a weary few days for the man, his son and the horse, and much land had been covered. The skies had been leaden from the start, blackened, relentless and unceasing, it seemed in the task of soaking everything beneath.

He pulled his cloak tighter around himself, making sure to give some cover to the boy and horse, and set off on the last of the journey to home.

And no sooner had he negotiated the wet, eel-slippery cobbles and turned the corner to the street where his parents' home stood, when a blur of chocolate brown stalled him and the horse.

Daniel looked down and a pair of black eyes looked back at him, a stubby tail wagging in rapturous welcome.

'Finn! Daddy!' he said, craning round to look at his father. 'Finn is here to see us!'

'Daniel! He knew you were coming, he has been waiting for you all this time,' panted his aunt Kate, looking most unladylike with her green embroidered skirts and sepia petticoats all rucked up with the effort of chasing the dog.

'My Auntie Kate!' screeched Daniel delightedly, and she held up her arms to him and helped him out of the saddle, leading him by the hand into the dry warmth of the Quinn house. 'Tea and cake?' James heard Daniel ask hopefully, and his aunt's laughing reply as she swung the boy around and hugged him until he begged to be let down.

James dismounted the horse in one fluid movement, and seeing his mother approach went to her and pulled her to him in a hug.

'James,' she looked up at him, pushing the wet strands of hair that had escaped from under his hat out of his eyes.

'Hello, Mother,' James smiled and hugged her. And he felt comforted.

'Hello son,' she smiled back, and taking his face between her hands kissed him. 'Now away with you and freshen up. Your father is out seeing to a patient but we will eat soon.'

James's mother and father glanced at him and then at each other, as he continued his impassioned speech, while Daniel played with Kate upstairs. It all came tumbling out, his friendship with Catherine that seemed to be blossoming into love until her abrupt departure, his feelings for Carissa that grew stronger and seemed to take on a life of their own. He was tired, confused; he spent all of his time thinking, and it had got him nowhere. It was time for action, time to find Carissa and tell her how he felt about her, and he didn't care if people thought he could have made a better match.

Mother Quinn covered her son's hand with her own. She was secretly delighted, as she had grown very close to the girl and knew how good she was with her grandson. Her strength after her father died and her mother went to pieces won Mother Quinn's lifelong respect.

'Leave Daniel here with us, James,' she said. 'He must be so tired from your journey.'

'We had to come on such a journey, Mother, I must know,' he had stood up in his obvious haste to be off and she took pity on him. 'Besides, Daniel misses her too, and we had a grand adventure, the two of us, on our way here.'

'Son,' began Doctor Dara, but his wife hushed him, as their son looked out of the window, emotions playing over his face.

James's mind was on Carissa as he rode out through the city's fortifications, past the quays and genteel living, over the bridge and on to the rows of poor thatched cottages and unkempt streets that made up the Claddagh fishing village.

Untended boats floated idly at anchor in the cove and white swans floated gracefully on the grey water as he knocked at the door of the rough cottage that was once home to Carissa's mother.

There was no reply, and trying the handle, he found that the door was open. He stepped inside and his heart sank as he looked around and saw that it was deserted. It had not been lived in for some time, as dust motes danced in the light and spiders made their homes in the dark corners.

James walked to the Spanish Arch and stood facing the Claddagh with his back against the stone wall. He turned and looked at it.

He found the loose stone easily enough, and he freed it from its place. Marguerite and James's wall, their stone, their hiding place for love notes through the years.

He placed the stone on the ground and reached into his pocket, his fingers brushing against the fabric that lay within, the scarlet ribbon. James took it out of his pocket and kissed it sweetly, reverently. He put the scarlet ribbon in a linen pouch and placed it in the recess in the wall before pushing the stone back, making sure that it was secure.

He turned to face Claddagh again, and as the sun sank, setting the water on fire, he whispered goodbye to Marguerite, his heart.

'I think Daniel and I will return to Dublin tomorrow,' James said to his mother and father over breakfast the following morning. He was bleary eyed and impatient and his head thumped, as he had tossed and turned the night away.

'I am sorry you did not find Carissa, James,' replied Doctor Dara. 'Since you are here today, perhaps you would do me a small favour? Thank you.

'I need you to visit my herbal woman, Mairin, in Barna, for fresh stocks for my medications cabinet. Perhaps you could take Daniel; the sea air will do him good. Here, I will make you a list of what I need.'

Once James and Daniel had left, Doctor Dara and Mother Quinn sat together, holding hands.

'Do you not think we should have told him?' she asked.

'My darling wife, I love every inch of you. But sometimes, your own darling boy has to make decisions for himself.'

She sighed deeply.

'We have done all we can now, my love, and then we will be here for him, always.'

She smiled at her husband. 'And hopefully, it will all come good.'

'Come here, woman,' he grabbed her and held her close to him, thanking the day that she was sent into his life. They sat among their thoughts, content in their embrace.

The horse knew his way well and needed no urging to follow the seashore and out into the tiny fishing village. James turned the horse's head and then they were on the well-worn track to Mairin's house. She waved to them as she saw them approach, hand on her lower back as she had been tending to her plants.

'It is good to see you again, James. And this must be Daniel. Your grandfather has told me much of you, so I am delighted to meet you.'

James eased himself off the horse and lifted Daniel down.

'Run along to my cottage, young man, there are some sweet things on the table, you may have one,' and she smiled at his retreating back and words of thanks thrown over his shoulder.

'Ah James, let me give you a present of some lily of the valley water, as, by the look of you, I fear your heart is in need of nourishment. Yes indeed,' she peered at his face intently. 'Now I should go and find your boy and make sure my cakes aren't all eaten!'

James turned to admire the garden and heard Daniel shouting.

He looked around, and there was Carissa, arms outstretched to catch the running child, gathering him tight to her when he reached her.

James walked to her, like a man in a dream, and she stood looking up at him, Daniel's hand in hers.

'Hello,' he said and cursed himself for his tongue being tied so, when all he wanted to do was profess his love for her. He tried again. 'What are you doing here?' No better, his brain admonished him.

'Mairin has agreed to let me be apprentice to her. I have always wanted to learn about plants and flowers and herbs that can heal and help – ever since my own poor mother never regained a smile on her face or a twinkle in her eye after the death of my father. And when Daniel was so ill, I swore that if he recovered I would never again be so helpless,' she replied, hurting, hating him yet desperate for him to take her into his arms.

'Carissa,' he began, startled that she had grown so much and that he had seemingly turned back into the awkward adolescent boy that he once was. Galway suited her far more than the fancy dresses and manners of Dublin. She was beautiful, and the words dried in his mouth.

'James, I cannot,' she replied and turned to go inside, still holding Daniel's hand, his sweet little face bright with the anticipation of the nearby confections.

'Wait!' he shouted, his voice booming in the tranquil garden.

She turned to look at him and he knew that he could not falter now.

'Carissa. Carissa, I would lay down my life for you.'

Her eyes filled with tears and she let go of the child's hand. Daniel ran into the kitchen, humming happily, thoughts of the sweets that waited there filling his mind.

James took a small step towards her. He took the hand that Daniel had so recently dropped. It was warm and small in his own.

'I would lay down my life for you,' he repeated, looking into her eyes.

She sighed.

'Carissa, let me read you something that I wrote for you. I started it, but was never really able to find the words to finish it and give it to you, so it has lingered on the desk in my study ever since.'

He took the piece of paper out of his pocket with his free hand and he read: 'My love. When I close my eyes I see your sweet face, and long for your gentle touch.'

Carissa's eyes filled with tears. She remembered leaving the letter in James's study that day and peeking at the sheet of paper on his desk. She assumed the note was meant for Catherine and she could feel her heart breaking through her chest, there and then, before she fled. Now that she knew it had been meant for her all along she felt sadness for the time wasted and also a deep, abiding peace and happiness.

She smiled up at him through the veil of her tears and he took her in his arms and held her close.

23

A meal for an infant

Cut a manchet of yeast bread of the highest quality into rounds. Dip these rounds into a mix of rich cream, six beaten eggs, nutmeg and sugar, and once they are wet through, fry them in sweet butter but keep them soft. Serve them up with sugar and butter, and cut small so the child may not choke.

Quinn Household Recipes and Remedies Book

DUBLIN, 1742

James Quinn walked the quiet Sunday noon streets of Dublin. He had been called out to a birth the previous night and he had just left a beaming father, delighted mother, and healthy baby girl. It had been a hard birth and a difficult time for everyone involved, so he was especially pleased for the new family. He smiled as he remembered, and pulled his coat a little tighter around him as the late-September air had a definite hint of a cold winter to come about it, but cold or no, this was coming up on his favourite time of the year.

The leaves were turning and the sky was bright blue. His dark hair gleamed as the sun caught it, and the faded warmth of the fiery orb caressed his back like a lover's embrace as he turned a corner to walk up by St Audoen's church. He would rub the lucky stone, he decided, in the hope that things would keep going his way – he had not felt so good in a long time.

He put down his pannier of instruments and stared up to the sky, which looked as if it had been painted in broad brush strokes by a master artist, so perfect it appeared.

Carissa stood at the front door of James Quinn's home and hugged her sister Aileen.

'Thank you again, Aileen, this is working out well I think.'

Aileen looked at her, happy and beaming with the way things were in her life since that day in Barna, the story of which she told over and over again. Carissa was learning the craft of herbalism from a woman here in Dublin, recommended by Mairin.

Since her relationship with James Quinn was moving on to a deeper level, it was no longer seemly for Carissa to spend nights in his home. So Aileen walked every evening from Sarah and Bernard Lynch's house, where she was still employed, to swap places with her sister. She returned every morning and Carissa once again took over the care of Daniel during the daytime.

'I will see you later,' Aileen bade her sister goodbye and pulled her coat tighter around her to keep out the chill in the air.

Carissa closed the door and went back inside to play with Daniel.

A few moments later, Peg looked in on the two of them, smiling as she saw them enjoying each other's company. She was glad that Carissa could find time to read up on herbs in the evenings and keep her days free for James's young son.

When his neck began to complain at being held at such an awkward angle for so long, James Quinn lowered his eyes from the sky and rolled his head to ease the tension.

He picked up his pannier and walked along the path to the church. The heavy, studded door was still open after earlier services, and the smell of incense and extinguished candles peppered the air.

He stopped and breathed in the warm scents and stillness before walking up the aisle, past the alabaster statues standing sentinel. He sat on a richly waxed pew, medical bag at his feet, and closed his eyes, allowing his mind to wander freely.

It tripped over the memories, never lingering too long on anything hurtful that he would previously have worried over until the pain was too much to bear, but unlike a rotten molar could never be ripped from him in a last agonising wrench thereafter freeing him from the persistent, hateful throb.

He breathed out. His life was so much better now, and though he would never forget Marguerite, he felt more at peace, as he hoped she was. He smiled.

Andre Moreau held his wife's hand as the carriage trundled its way along Dublin's cobbles towards James Quinn's home for the lunch that had been planned for them. Their daughter Lisette sat in his lap, and he kissed her cheek while sweeping her curls off her forehead with his other hand.

'We will be there soon, my love, I am so excited to see James once again!' Andre was full of delight and as excited as a child at the thought of seeing his friend.

Avril smiled at him; his happiness was infectious, and it was a relief, in truth, to be starting a new life with him and Lisette away from the gossips of Paris. She had not told Andre, but people avoided her in the street and hissed cruel things to her back as she passed. They were never brave enough to say anything to her face. She stared out the window at the passing scenery, interested to visit a new city, full of plans for settling into their new life in New Orleans.

Andre hummed under his breath and dandled his little girl. He hugged her to him, and she squawked a little indignantly as his embrace was too tight. He laughed out loud with love for the child.

'See, Lisette, there is a horse!' he said to the infant, making a whinnying sound, and she looked up at him with her eyes round as saucers and did her best to copy the noise he had just made.

'Avril, did you hear that? We have a genius on our hands!'

His happiness was her happiness, and Avril reached over and kissed the man who had made her so very content, had rescued her from an imperfect life and made a gift of the vision and soon-to-be reality of a new one.

'I love you, Avril,' he said, thinking he had never seen her look so beautiful.

They kissed again, and the little girl, cross to not be at the centre of their universe for even just one moment, whimpered her displeasure. Andre laughed and moved her so that she sat between them, and the three shared an embrace.

James Quinn opened his eyes, feeling deeply relaxed and at ease. He sat a while longer and then picked up his bag and walked to the lucky stone that his father had rubbed so long ago. His footfalls echoed around the church as he made his way to the charm. The slab's granite surface was rubbed so smooth that it nearly shone, after so many believers had touched it with their fingers over the years. James ran his hand over the cold, hard surface and then let his finger trace the Celtic whorls carved into the stone.

He remembered the day that he had been here with his father, and how he had tried to reach him with his words and then his embraces, the look on his face, pleading and sad and earnest. The horrible moment the choir had started to sing the song from his own, sweet, tender marriage to the love of his life, Marguerite.

Catherine Cavendish fretted and played with the fringe on her shawl, letting the silky tassels run through her fingers.

'Oh Father, don't you think we should have said that we were coming? Isn't it rude to turn up unannounced like this?'

'Nonsense, my dear!' replied Sir Alan. 'Besides, it would have been rude not to come for a quick visit, seeing as it is on our way to Drumaline.' He sniffed, 'although, for the life of me, I don't see why your husband is not with us, given your condition.'

Catherine looked down at her growing belly. She cupped it tenderly and felt the baby move within. She was six months pregnant now and glad the sickness that had plagued her in the early days had disappeared. She sighed and looked out of the window at the Dublin streets on the way to James Quinn's home. She had not travelled this way for some time, or been back to the house since the performance of *Messiah*. Her cousin Edward had rescued her that evening. A tight smile played with her lips, trying to tug the corners of her mouth up but failing.

'I don't see why he had to go on yet another hunt today, that's all,' continued her father, somewhat huffily.

'Father! Honestly,' cried Catherine, 'what Edward does is not under my control, just as what you do is not under my control.' She looked at him crossly, features softening as she saw his love for her there.

'I know, my dear, forgive me. I just want the best for you. And besides, I am getting very eager to meet my first grandchild! I doubt your sister Alice and that new man of hers ever plan to present me with one, you know.'

'Father!' Catherine replied. 'What a scandalous thing to say,' though she smiled to herself; she couldn't see her sister with a baby to take care of as she needed to be petted and cosseted constantly herself.

James Quinn stood quietly.

'James,' his name was whispered so softly that he wasn't sure that he had actually heard it. 'James,' it came again, indistinct, and he felt a love so pure and shining that it warmed him from the inside out. He stood for a moment longer to embrace the joy deep within himself. He smiled and rubbed the stone, wishing good things for himself, his family, his friends and his patients, before making his way back to the open door of the church. He stood for a moment and gazed out at the glorious day.

He stepped aside for an elderly lady as she made her way to prayer, smiling at her as she passed, and looked back into the church once more, before making his way back down the path and on to the street. Pannier in hand, he continued his walk to his home in St Patrick's Close, which was only a short distance from the church, the song in his heart taken up by the birds in the trees and from there to Heaven.

During his walk home, James Quinn wondered what Carissa and Daniel would be doing, and what time his good friend Andre would arrive with Avril and their year-old baby girl Lisette.

The trees still had a canopy of leaves, even though these were drying and nearly ready to fall and carpet the streets, and James gazed as the sunlight made them transparently beautiful. He turned the corner, walked towards home, and came to a stop: the morning's ethereal flights of fancy were extinguished when he saw three carriages outside his house.

The second would be Laurence Stone's, whom he'd invited to lunch to meet Andre, but whose was the third? He hurried towards the front door, eager to discover who else was here and to meet again with Andre and Avril, when he was halted by the banging at the lower front window. He looked through the window and saw a small infant beaming at him. He crouched down and held his hand against the child's tiny one, glass separating them. The baby girl gave him a gappy, gummy smile and it suddenly dawned on him that this must be Lisette. He smiled back.

He straightened up, waved to the child, and went to go inside to greet his friends. His hand had just reached for the doorknob when the smile of welcome left his face and he felt a gnawing, growing thought expand in his head. Heart thumping, legs trembling, James Quinn walked back to the window and crouched down again, kneeling on the cold ground, not minding that his knees were in the dirt or that his coat was trailing on the ground. Lisette was delighted to see him again, to continue the game, and she placed her small hand on the window pane once more. He held his shaking hand against hers, glass separating them.

The baby girl gave him a gappy, gummy smile and he saw that Lisette was the image of Daniel. He smiled back.

24

To ensure a safe voyage by sea
Take from all of these a large dried sprig: lavender, sage, thyme, lemon balm, hyssop and peppermint, and add a handful of cloves of garlic. Place in a jar and cover with apple cider vinegar and put a lid on the top. Let the jar sit in a cool place for six weeks and then strain off the herbs and garlic and pour into a vessel with a stopper. Take the mixture several times daily, add a drop to your food, and put some of the liquid on a soft cloth and clean around you. It is sure to ward off any illnesses, large or small.

Quinn Household Recipes and Remedies Book

To say that the lunch was strained was putting it mildly, thought James as he waved off Laurence Stone.

His mentor had made small talk before getting deep into discussion with Andre about man-midwifery in Paris, and his plans for New Orleans. Catherine and her father, though uninvited, filled any gaps in the conversation and James blessed their untimely arrival. Catherine smiled at James across the table, eyebrow raised in question as she looked from Daniel to Lisette. All James could do was shrug in return. Sir Alan seemed very interested in the American venture; he was no doubt hoping to find another way to make his money grow.

Peg cosseted the children, Avril chatted contentedly, but it was Carissa that James was most worried about. He saw her confusion and hurt as he engaged in easy, light-hearted conversation with Avril and made much of Lisette, who was very taken with Daniel. James sighed and turned to go back inside when Andre came out with Lisette in his arms and Daniel by the hand.

'Let us take a walk. You look like a man who could do with the wise advice of myself,' he joked.

Inside the house, Avril sat and rested by the fire, telling Peg of the current fashions in Paris, while Sir Alan dozed. Catherine saw Carissa's face set in anger and walked over to her.

'Carissa, dear,' she said sweetly, 'may I have a word with you?'

Carissa followed Catherine into the hallway.

'Carissa,' she began, 'there was no need to sit with a face like thunder over lunch. You put me quite off my food.'

'How can you say that?' Carissa hissed, 'I would be a fool not to see that the Frenchwoman's child is also James's!'

'Lower your voice and stop making such a scene, you silly little girl! Do you really think you are good enough for James?'

Carissa's face crumpled and Catherine softened. 'I am sorry, Carissa, I did not mean that. It is this pregnancy; I feel so tired and often agitated. But come, does it really matter if Lisette is James's child?'

'I suppose next you will be telling me that he is also your child's father!' started Carissa, and then stopped as she saw the truth in Catherine's eyes. 'Oh no, say it is not true!'

she pleaded and hung on to the Englishwoman's arm.

'Carissa,' Catherine put her arms around her.

'I knew it!' Carissa whirled out of Catherine's grasp. 'And you are all content to make a complete fool out of me.'

'Carissa, dear, it was not like that.'

'I saw him, did you know that?' her finger pointed at Catherine, and it trembled. 'I saw your husband Edward at the picnic. He was with Charles, holding his hands; I knew it was not right.'

'My husband may love me less than his male friends,' Catherine shrugged, 'it does not matter to me. We are very close. He was delighted that he did not have to cover me to obtain an heir, hopefully a son. Unfortunately, I have discovered that my money covers his gambling debts. Again, what does it matter? We have a good life together and most importantly I have a legal father for my child.'

'You are very cold-hearted, Catherine Cavendish!' Carissa turned to go.

'Don't you mean Countess? Carissa, not so fast. Do not cry, dear, or make me cut your stays and bring you the smelling salts so you get over your fit. This is real life; we women must use our wiles to get what we want. If you still want James, you must fight for him, especially as he saw you so unhappy at the table.

'Calm yourself, take a deep breath, dry your eyes, put on scent, do your hair again, and greet him with a smile as if none of this matters. And by the way, he does not know he is father to my child. I would prefer to keep it that way.'

'So,' said Andre.

'So,' replied James, shoulders slumped in dejection.

'James,' roared Andre, 'your face is a picture!'

James watched his friend dissolve into laughter and couldn't help but laugh along too.

'Carissa,' he began.

'Carissa will be fine, James. If she wants to be with you she will, surprise child or no.'

James eyed his friend sheepishly, putting his finger between his collar and his neck. 'I didn't know. I knew that something was amiss the day that Avril and I parted at Notre Dame, but I had no idea what it was.' He cleared his throat.

Andre smiled and put his arm around James. He handed Lisette to him. 'Avril told me about that. I met her not long after your departure. You may have provided the seed to enable Lisette to grow, and in that respect she is your daughter. But she is mine more than yours,' and he picked Daniel up in his arms.

'She is beautiful,' breathed James.

'You know,' said Andre, pausing for a moment, 'if you were to come with us we would all be one big happy family.'

'To New Orleans?'

'Where else? New Orleans: new, exciting, full of adventure. We could become the Gregoires of America, my friend.'

'What about the rest of my family?'

'Bring them all – even Peg, marvellous woman – in a year's time, when Avril and I are established.'

Lisette, tired, snuggled into James's chest and closed her eyes. He bent his head over hers and revelled in the smell of her wispy baby hair.

'Come, James, we could be happy there. Daniel, would you like to go on a big ship?'

'Yes! Like Robinson Crusoe?' he stumbled over the words and both men laughed, the child joining in.

'But I hate travelling by sea with a vengeance,' said James.

'Come now, no excuses. The trade winds would be at our backs; it would be a fine crossing. What do you say?'

James Quinn looked at his children and then Andre.

'I think we could be happy there,' he smiled.

Historical Note

Some of the characters in *The Scarlet Ribbon* are fictional, but Gregoire the Elder and Gregoire the Younger taught at the Hotel Dieu. William Smellie, called Smyley in this book, was a prominent man-midwife in London. Bartholomew Mosse and Fielding Ould were man-midwives in Dublin.

The medical procedures, case notes, and remedies related here are historically accurate. In the eighteenth century, the practice of man-midwifery met with criticism and opposition.

The King's Head, still a pub, and Lynch's Castle, now a bank, are in Galway city. The Claddagh, Spanish Arch and St Nicholas' church are also in Galway. St Auden's church and St Anne's church are in Dublin city. The Hotel Dieu is in Paris, just beside Notre Dame. After its demise in 1859, the site of The New Spring Gardens, Vauxhall, London, was divided up into 300 building plots. During the Blitz, the site was cleared, and is now a park.